RSC School Shakespeare

Series consultant: Emma Smith
Professor of Shakespeare Studies
Hertford College, University of Oxford

MUCH ADO ABOUT NOTHING

OXFORD
UNIVERSITY PRESS

OXFORD
UNIVERSITY PRESS

Great Clarendon Street, Oxford, OX2 6DP,
United Kingdom

Oxford University Press is a department of the University of Oxford.
It furthers the University's objective of excellence in research, scholarship,
and education by publishing worldwide. Oxford is a registered trade mark of Oxford
University Press in the UK and in certain other countries

British Library Cataloguing in Publication Data

Data available

ISBN 978-019-836594-5

10 9 8 7 6 5 4 3 2 1

Printed in Great Britain by Bell and Bain Ltd., Glasgow

Acknowledgements

Cover and performance images © Royal Shakespeare Company 2016

Much Ado About Nothing photographs by Simon Annand (2006), Ellie Kurttz (2012) and
Manuel Harlan (2014).

p196 (middle): Janet Faye Hastings / Shutterstock; p196 (bottom): mashakotcur /
Shutterstock; p197 (top right): 19th era / Alamy Stock Photo; p197 (middle right): Granger,
NYC. / Alamy Stock Photo; p197 (middle left): © National Portrait Gallery, London; p200:
DEA PICTURE LIBRARY / Getty Images; p207: Pictorial Press Ltd / Alamy Stock Photo

Layout by Justin Hoffmann at Pixelfox

Contents

Introduction to
RSC School Shakespeare

The RSC approach

The classroom as rehearsal room

All the work of RSC Education is underpinned by the artistic practice of the Royal Shakespeare Company (RSC). In particular, we make very strong connections between the rehearsal rooms in which our actors and directors work and the classrooms in which you learn. Rehearsal rooms are essentially places of exploration and shared discovery, in which a company of actors and their director work together to bring Shakespeare's plays to life. To do this successfully they need to have a deep understanding of the text, to get the language 'in the body' and to be open to a range of interpretive possibilities and choices. The ways in which they do this are both active and playful, connecting mind, voice and body.

Becoming a company

To do this we begin by deliberately building a spirit of one group with a shared purpose – this is about 'us' rather than 'me'. We often do this with games that warm up our brains, voices and bodies, and we continue to build this spirit through a scheme of work that includes shared, collaborative tasks that depend on and value everyone's contributions. The ways in which the activities work in this edition encourage discussion, speculation and questioning: there is rarely one right answer. This process requires and develops critical thinking.

Making the world of the play

In rehearsals at the RSC, we explore the whole world of the play: we tackle the language, characters and motivation, setting, plot and themes. By 'standing in the shoes' of the characters and exploring the world of the play, you will be engaged fully: head, eyes, ears, hands, bodies and hearts are involved in actively interpreting the play. In grappling with scenes and speeches, you are also actively grappling with the themes and ideas in the play, experiencing them from the points of view of the different characters.

The language is central to our discoveries

We place the language in the plays at the core of everything we do. Active, playful approaches can make Shakespeare's words vivid, accessible and enjoyable. His language has the power to excite and delight all of us.

In the rehearsal room, the RSC uses social and historical context in order to deepen understanding of the world of the play. The company is engaged in a 'conversation across time', inviting audiences to consider what a play means to us now and what it meant to us then. We hope that the activities in this edition will offer you an opportunity to join that conversation.

The activities require close, critical reading and encourage you to make informed interpretive choices about language, character and motivation, themes and plot. The work is rooted in speaking and listening to Shakespeare's words and to each other's ideas in order to help embrace and unlock this extraordinary literary inheritance.

Jacqui O'Hanlon
Director of Education
Royal Shakespeare Company

The Royal Shakespeare Theatre

Using *RSC School Shakespeare*

As you open each double page, you will see the script of the play on the right-hand page. On the left-hand page is a series of features that will help you connect with and explore William Shakespeare's play *Much Ado About Nothing* and the world in which Shakespeare lived.

Those features are:

Summary

At the top of every left-hand page is a summary of what happens on the facing page to help you understand the action.

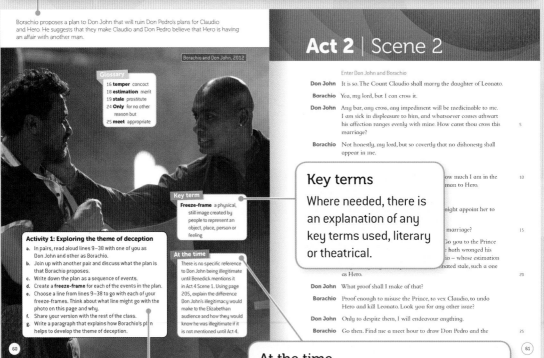

Key terms

Where needed, there is an explanation of any key terms used, literary or theatrical.

Activity

Every left-hand page includes at least one activity that is inspired by RSC rehearsal room practice.

At the time

There are social and historical research tasks, so that you can use knowledge from the time the play was written to help you interpret the text of the play. The social and historical information can be found on pages 196–207 of this edition.

Did you know?

For every scene, we have provided a piece of information about the work of RSC actors, directors and designers. We hope this helps you understand more about how the RSC go about rehearsing a play for performance onstage.

Glossary

Where needed, there is a glossary that explains words from the play that may be unfamiliar and cannot be worked out in context.

Don Pedro, Claudio and Leonato leave Benedick alone. He shares with the audience his thoughts and feelings about Beatrice, and decides that he loves her. Beatrice comes in and tells him it is dinner time.

Did you know?

Actors often physically explore the punctuation in a speech to help them connect with the way their character is thinking and feeling.

Glossary

182–183 **no such matter** there will be nothing in it
184 **a dumb show** speechless
185 **sadly** seriously
187 **full bent** fully stretched (like an archer's bow)
196 **horribly** totally
201–202 **career of his humour** pursuit of his mood

Activity 7: Exploring punctuation

a. Read lines 185–205. As you read aloud, stand up on the first full stop, sit down on the next one and then continue standing up or sitting down every time you come to a full stop. Treat the question marks in the same way. When you come to a comma, stamp your foot.

b. Join up with a partner and discuss what impact the use of punctuation has in this speech. The punctuation is an indicator of a character moving from one thought to another. What state of mind would you say Benedick is in? How do you think he is feeling during this speech? Why might that be?

c. Write a paragraph or two explaining what you think Benedick's state of mind is at this stage in the play. Use evidence from lines 185–205 in your writing.

76

Benedick, 2014

Act 2 | Scene 3

Leonato My lord, will you walk? Dinner is ready.

Claudio [Aside] If he do not dote on her upon this, I will never trust my expectation.

Don Pedro [Aside] Let there be the same net spread for her, and that must your daughter and her gentlewomen carry. The sport will be when they hold one an opinion of another's dotage, but no such matter. That's the scene that I would see, which will be merely a dumb show. Let us send her to call him in to dinner. 180

Exeunt Don Pedro, Claudio and Leonato

Benedick This can be no trick. The conference was sadly borne. They have the truth of this from Hero. They seem to pity the lady. It seems her affections have their full bent. Love me? Why, it must 185
be requited. I hear how I am censured. They say I will bear myself proudly if I perceive the love come from her. They say too that she will rather die than give any sign of affection. I did 190
never think to marry. I must not seem proud. Happy are they that hear their detractions and can put them to mending. They say the lady is fair. 'Tis a truth, I can bear them witness. And virtuous. 'Tis so, I cannot reprove it. And wise, but for loving me. 195
By my troth, it is no addition to her wit, nor no great argument of her folly, for I will be horribly in love with her. I may chance have some odd quirks and remnants of wit broken on me because I have railed so long against marriage, but doth not the appetite alter? A man loves the meat in his youth that he 200
cannot endure in his age. Shall quips and sentences and these paper bullets of the brain awe a man from the career of his humour? No. The world must be peopled. When I said I would die a bachelor, I did not think I should live till I were married. Here comes Beatrice. By this day, she's a fair lady. I do spy some 205
marks of love in her.

Enter Beatrice

Beatrice Against my will I am sent to bid you come in to dinner.

Benedick Fair Beatrice, I thank you for your pains.

77

RSC performance photographs

Every left-hand page includes at least one photograph from an RSC production of the play. Some of the activities make direct use of the production photographs. The photographs illustrate the action, bringing to life the text on the facing page. They also include a caption that identifies the character or event, together with the date of the RSC production.

The play in performance

A popular success

We believe that *Much Ado About Nothing* was written towards the end of the 16th century and enjoyed many performances, which means it must have been popular with audiences.

At the Royal Shakespeare Company (RSC), we have staged countless productions of *Much Ado About Nothing* and each time they are completely different. Shakespeare's plays are packed full of questions and challenges for the director, designer and acting company to solve. The clues to finding the answers are always somewhere in the text, but the possibilities for interpretation are infinite.

A place of possibilities

One of the most interesting questions a director needs to answer about any scene is whether it is public or private. In *Much Ado About Nothing*, we have the first meeting between Beatrice and Benedick; exploring which of their lines are played publicly and which are played privately radically alters the mood and meaning of the scene. That's what happens in the rehearsal room. Actors and their director try out different ways of playing scenes informed always by the clues that Shakespeare gives them; they effectively become text detectives, mining the language for clues to help inform their performance choices.

We have taken all of the ways of working of our actors and directors and set them alongside the text of *Much Ado About Nothing* which, together with the other titles in the series, offers a great introduction to Shakespeare's world and work.

An actor once described the rehearsal room to me as a 'place of possibilities'. I think that's a wonderful way of thinking about a classroom too and it's what we hope the *RSC School Shakespeare* editions help to create.

Jacqui O'Hanlon
Director of Education
Royal Shakespeare Company

The play at a glance

Every scene in a play presents a challenge to the actors and their director in terms of how to stage it. There are certain key scenes in a play that directors need to pay special attention to because they contain really significant events. Here are some of the key scenes in *Much Ado About Nothing*.

The Prince and his followers arrive (Act 1 Scene 1)

The war is over. Don Pedro, Prince of Aragon, arrives in Messina with his followers, Benedick and Claudio, and his half-brother Don John. Leonato, Governor of Messina, invites the men to stay. Claudio falls in love with Hero, Leonato's daughter. Benedick and Beatrice, Leonato's niece, exchange witty insults.

Don John, Borachio and Conrad plot against Hero (Act 2 Scene 2)

After the date for Claudio and Hero's wedding is set, Borachio, Don John and Conrad plot to fool Don Pedro and Claudio into believing that Hero is unfaithful. Borachio plans to stage a scene at Margaret's window where she will pretend to be Hero as he woos her.

The others trick Benedick and Beatrice (Act 2 Scene 3 / Act 3 Scene 1)

The others plot to make Benedick and Beatrice fall in love with each other, by a trick in which Benedick will overhear his friends talking of Beatrice's supposed secret love for him, and vice versa.

Claudio and Hero's wedding (Act 4 Scene 1)

Claudio accuses Hero of being unfaithful during the marriage ceremony. She faints and on the advice of the Friar, who is convinced of her innocence, Leonato announces that she is dead. Benedick and Beatrice confess their love for one another and she demands that he should kill Claudio.

A happy ending (Act 5 Scene 1 / Act 5 Scene 3)

Borachio, arrested by the foolish constable Dogberry and the Watch, confesses to Don Pedro and Claudio. They realise that Hero was innocent and mourn her 'death'. Claudio promises to make amends to Leonato: he is required to marry Leonato's 'niece'. At the wedding, Leonato's 'niece' is revealed to be Hero. Beatrice agrees to marry Benedick.

Much Ado About Nothing

Leonato, Governor of Messina

Beatrice, Leonato's niece

Hero, Leonato's daughter

Antonio, Leonato's brother, uncle to Beatrice and Hero

Margaret, gentlewoman

Ursula, gentlewoman

Don Pedro, Prince of Aragon

Benedick, friend and follower of Don Pedro

Claudio, friend and follower of Don Pedro

Don John, Don Pedro's illegitimate brother

Borachio, friend and follower of Don John

Conrad, friend and follower of Don John

Balthasar, singer and servant to Don Pedro

Boy, servant to Benedick

Friar Francis

Dogberry, Constable in charge of The Watch

Verges, Dogberry's deputy

Sexton

The Watch

Messenger

Leonato, Governor of Messina receives the news that Don Pedro, Prince of Aragon and his men are approaching Messina on their return from the wars. The Prince (Don Pedro) has honoured Claudio for his bravery.

Leonato and the Messenger, 2006

Glossary

24 **Mountanto** an upward thrust in sword fighting

Activity 1: Exploring active listening

a. In small groups, decide who will play Leonato, Messenger and Beatrice. Stand with your backs to each other and read aloud lines 1–26. Listen carefully to each other.

b. Read the lines aloud again, but this time repeat out loud the last few words that you heard the previous speaker say before you say your own lines. Use what you have heard to help you to deliver your own lines more convincingly.

c. Write a summary of lines 1–26 from the point of view of the character you have been playing.

d. Swap your summaries in your groups and pick out any differences in the characters' attitudes to the news that the soldiers are returning.

Did you know?

The **director** and actors at the RSC typically spend six weeks in full-time rehearsals for a play like *Much Ado About Nothing*. They spend time putting it into their own words and then get up on their feet to explore Shakespeare's original text.

Key term

Director the person who enables the practical and creative interpretation of a dramatic script, and ultimately brings together everybody's ideas in a way that engages the audience with the play

Act 1 | Scene 1

Enter Leonato, Hero and Beatrice, with a Messenger

Leonato   I learn in this letter that Don Pedro of Aragon comes this night
to Messina.

Messenger   He is very near by this. He was not three leagues off when
I left him.

Leonato   How many gentlemen have you lost in this action?   5

Messenger   But few of any sort, and none of name.

Leonato   A victory is twice itself when the achiever brings home full
numbers. I find here that Don Pedro hath bestowed much
honour on a young Florentine called Claudio.

Messenger   Much deserved on his part and equally remembered by Don   10
Pedro. He hath borne himself beyond the promise of his age,
doing in the figure of a lamb the feats of a lion. He hath indeed
better bettered expectation than you must expect of me to tell
you how.

Leonato   He hath an uncle here in Messina will be very much glad of it.   15

Messenger   I have already delivered him letters, and there appears much
joy in him, even so much that joy could not show itself modest
enough without a badge of bitterness.

Leonato   Did he break out into tears?

Messenger   In great measure.   20

Leonato   A kind overflow of kindness; there are no faces truer than those
that are so washed. How much better is it to weep at joy than to
joy at weeping?

Beatrice   I pray you, is Signor Mountanto returned from the wars or no?

Beatrice wonders whether Signor Benedick is returning from the wars and then tells everybody what she thinks of him.

Beatrice and Benedick, 2014

Activity 2: Exploring the character of Benedick

a. In small groups, decide who will play Leonato, Messenger, Hero and Beatrice. Read aloud lines 27–67.

b. Write a list of all the things that Beatrice says about Benedick in this section.

c. Using modern English, write down one characteristic that sums up each of the things on your list. For example, when Beatrice says he is 'governed with one [wit]', you could write 'unintelligent'.

d. Choose one characteristic each. Create an individual **statue** that shows that characteristic of Benedick as Beatrice sees him.

e. Choose one line from lines 27–67 that is most relevant to your statue. Bring your statue to life as you speak the line.

f. Write a paragraph that explains which of the statues in your group was the most effective and why.

Glossary

30 **bills** poster adverts

30–31 **the flight** an archery competition

32 **bird-bolt** blunt wooden arrow used by fools and children

33 **killed and eaten** It was believed that eating the body of an enemy made you brave and strong

39 **valiant trencherman** hearty eater

44 **stuffed man** scarecrow

49–50 **five wits** People believed there were five mental abilities: imagination, fancy, judgement, memory and common sense

Key term

Statue like a freeze-frame but usually of a single character

Messenger I know none of that name, lady. There was none such in the   25
army of any sort.

Leonato What is he that you ask for, niece?

Hero My cousin means Signor Benedick of Padua.

Messenger O he's returned, and as pleasant as ever he was.

Beatrice He set up his bills here in Messina, and challenged Cupid at the   30
flight, and my uncle's fool, reading the challenge, subscribed for
Cupid, and challenged him at the bird-bolt. I pray you, how
many hath he killed and eaten in these wars? But how many
hath he killed? For indeed I promised to eat all of his killing.

Leonato Faith, niece, you tax Signor Benedick too much. But he'll be   35
meet with you, I doubt it not.

Messenger He hath done good service, lady, in these wars.

Beatrice You had musty victual, and he hath holp to eat it. He's a very
valiant trencherman. He hath an excellent stomach.

Messenger And a good soldier too, lady.   40

Beatrice And a good soldier to a lady, but what is he to a lord?

Messenger A lord to a lord, a man to a man, stuffed with all honourable
virtues.

Beatrice It is so, indeed. He is no less than a stuffed man. But for the
stuffing – well, we are all mortal.   45

Leonato You must not, sir, mistake my niece. There is a kind of merry war
betwixt Signor Benedick and her. They never meet but there's a
skirmish of wit between them.

Beatrice Alas, he gets nothing by that. In our last conflict four of his five
wits went halting off, and now is the whole man governed with   50
one. So that if he have wit enough to keep himself warm, let
him bear it for a difference between himself and his horse, for
it is all the wealth that he hath left, to be known a reasonable
creature. Who is his companion now? He hath every month a
new sworn brother.   55

Don Pedro and his men arrive and Leonato welcomes them.

Don Pedro, Benedick, Claudio and Leonato, 2006

Glossary

58 **next block** newest wooden mould for shaping a hat

59 **books** good books

61 **squarer** fighter

Activity 3: Exploring 'as ifs'

a. In small groups, decide who will play Don Pedro, Leonato and Benedick. First, read aloud lines 73–87 as if the characters don't know each other very well and are awkward.

b. Then read aloud lines 73–87 as if the characters are old friends who are very comfortable with each other.

c. Join up with another group and discuss which version felt most appropriate and why.

d. Share your work with another group. Discuss what was effective in each performance.

e. Look at the photo on this page and discuss which moment you think it shows and why.

f. One of the **themes** of the play is male and female relationships and the roles of men and women. Some people think that Shakespeare originally planned this scene with Hero's mother (Leonato's wife) present. How would lines 73–87 be different if she were there?

Key term

Theme the main ideas explored in a piece of literature, e.g. the themes of love and marriage, male and female relationships, deception, loyalty and honour might be considered key themes of *Much Ado About Nothing*

Did you know?

'Try it as if…' is a phrase that is sometimes used by the director in rehearsals to encourage the actors to try out a scene in different ways, until they find the version that they all agree on.

Messenger Is't possible?

Beatrice Very easily possible. He wears his faith but as the fashion of his
hat: it ever changes with the next block.

Messenger I see, lady, the gentleman is not in your books.

Beatrice No; and he were, I would burn my study. But I pray you, who is   60
his companion? Is there no young squarer now that will make a
voyage with him to the devil?

Messenger He is most in the company of the right noble Claudio.

Beatrice O Lord, he will hang upon him like a disease. He is sooner
caught than the pestilence, and the taker runs presently mad.   65
God help the noble Claudio. If he have caught the Benedick, it
will cost him a thousand pound ere he be cured.

Messenger I will hold friends with you, lady.

Beatrice Do, good friend.

Leonato You'll ne'er run mad, niece.   70

Beatrice No, not till a hot January.

Messenger Don Pedro is approached.

Enter Don Pedro, Claudio, Benedick, Balthasar and Don John

Don Pedro Good Signor Leonato, you are come to meet your trouble? The
fashion of the world is to avoid cost, and you encounter it.

Leonato Never came trouble to my house in the likeness of your grace,   75
for trouble being gone, comfort should remain. But when you
depart from me, sorrow abides and happiness takes his leave.

Don Pedro You embrace your charge too willingly. I think this is
your daughter.

Leonato Her mother hath many times told me so.   80

Benedick Were you in doubt, sir, that you asked her?

Leonato Signor Benedick, no, for then were you a child.

Benedick, Hero, Claudio and Beatrice, 2006

Activity 4: Exploring the theme of male and female relationships

a. In pairs, discuss people you know who like to put each other down. Why do they do it?

b. Sit on a chair facing your partner and decide who will be 'A' and who will be 'B'. You must stay in contact with your chair throughout this activity, but you are allowed to move on it and around it. Student A makes a move to make themselves look better than Student B. For example, Student A could sit up straighter and give their partner a dirty look. Student B then answers by making a move that makes them look better than Student A. How far can you go before you can no longer 'top' your partner?

c. Read aloud lines 88–109 with one of you as Beatrice and the other as Benedick. Read the lines at the same time as making your moves from task b, using the words to put each other down.

d. Look at the photo on this page and discuss what each character's **body language** suggests.

e. Write a paragraph that explains how the use of **gesture**, **tone**, volume and **emphasis** add to our understanding of what is going on between Beatrice and Benedick, and to your understanding of the theme of male and female relationships.

Glossary

91 **meet** right (with a **pun** on 'meat')

106 **A bird of… beast of yours** my words sing like birdsong compared to your animal noises

109 **jade** a horse that refuses to go on

Key terms

Pun a play on words

Body language how we communicate feelings to each other using our bodies (including facial expressions) rather than words

Gesture a movement, often using the hands or head, to express a feeling or idea

Tone as in 'tone of voice'; expressing an attitude through how you say something

Emphasis stress given to words when speaking

Don Pedro You have it full, Benedick. We may guess by this what you are, being a man. Truly, the lady fathers herself. Be happy, lady, for you are like an honourable father.   85

Benedick If Signor Leonato be her father, she would not have his head on her shoulders for all Messina, as like him as she is.

Beatrice I wonder that you will still be talking, Signor Benedick. Nobody marks you.

Benedick What, my dear Lady Disdain! Are you yet living?   90

Beatrice Is it possible Disdain should die while she hath such meet food to feed it as Signor Benedick? Courtesy itself must convert to Disdain, if you come in her presence.

Benedick Then is courtesy a turncoat. But it is certain I am loved of all ladies, only you excepted. And I would I could find in my heart   95 that I had not a hard heart, for truly I love none.

Beatrice A dear happiness to women. They would else have been troubled with a pernicious suitor. I thank God and my cold blood, I am of your humour for that. I had rather hear my dog bark at a crow than a man swear he loves me.   100

Benedick God keep your ladyship still in that mind, so some gentleman or other shall 'scape a predestinate scratched face.

Beatrice Scratching could not make it worse, an 'twere such a face as yours were.

Benedick Well, you are a rare parrot-teacher.   105

Beatrice A bird of my tongue is better than a beast of yours.

Benedick I would my horse had the speed of your tongue, and so good a continuer. But keep your way, o' God's name, I have done.

Beatrice You always end with a jade's trick. I know you of old.

Don Pedro That is the sum of all, Leonato. Signor Claudio and Signor   110 Benedick, my dear friend Leonato hath invited you all. I tell him we shall stay here at the least a month and he heartily

Everyone, except Benedick and Claudio, leaves. When they are alone, Claudio brings up Hero, Leonato's daughter. They tell each other what they think of her.

Hero, 2006

Did you know?

Actors sometimes find it useful in rehearsals to create physical gestures that describe the meaning of the words they are saying. They do not use these in performance, but making the gestures helps them to explore every detail in the language their character is using.

Activity 5: Exploring different characters' views of love

a. In pairs, read aloud lines 121–141 with one of you as Claudio and the other as Benedick.

b. Pick out all the words that Claudio and Benedick use to describe Hero.

c. Stand up and create gestures to go with each word you have chosen. For example, for 'sweetest' in line 141, you might lick your fingers as if you are tasting something sweet.

d. Keep the same characters and read aloud lines 121–141 again, this time on your feet, using the gestures you have created.

e. Consider what you have found out about the ideal woman in Shakespeare's time from the 'At the time' box. Which character would you say was idealising Hero? Why do you think Shakespeare has put Benedick's opinion of Hero into this scene? What effect does it have putting the two points of view together?

f. Write notes on Hero as Claudio sees her in lines 121–141.

At the time

Using page 204, find out what ideas people held about the 'ideal' woman in Shakespeare's time. How do these compare with ideas about the 'ideal' woman today?

Glossary

128 **brown** She has brown hair

138 **flouting jack** character who does the opposite to what is expected

138–139 **Cupid... hare-finder** Cupid was blind and therefore could not find a hare, which is hard to see in its natural habitat

139 **Vulcan... carpenter** Vulcan was actually a blacksmith

prays some occasion may detain us longer. I dare swear he is no hypocrite, but prays from his heart.

Leonato   If you swear, my lord, you shall not be forsworn.   115

[To Don John] Let me bid you welcome, my lord. Being reconciled to the Prince your brother, I owe you all duty.

Don John   I thank you. I am not of many words, but I thank you.

Leonato   Please it your grace lead on?

Don Pedro   Your hand, Leonato. We will go together.   120

Exeunt all except Benedick and Claudio

Claudio   Benedick, didst thou note the daughter of Signor Leonato?

Benedick   I noted her not, but I looked on her.

Claudio   Is she not a modest young lady?

Benedick   Do you question me, as an honest man should do, for my simple true judgement, or would you have me speak after my custom,   125
as being a professed tyrant to their sex?

Claudio   No, I pray thee speak in sober judgement.

Benedick   Why, i' faith, methinks she's too low for a high praise, too brown for a fair praise and too little for a great praise. Only this commendation I can afford her, that were she other than she is,   130
she were unhandsome, and being no other but as she is, I do not like her.

Claudio   Thou think'st I am in sport. I pray thee tell me truly how thou lik'st her.

Benedick   Would you buy her that you inquire after her?   135

Claudio   Can the world buy such a jewel?

Benedick   Yea, and a case to put it into. But speak you this with a sad brow? Or do you play the flouting jack, to tell us Cupid is a good hare-finder and Vulcan a rare carpenter? Come, in what key shall a man take you to go in the song?   140

Benedick tells Claudio that he prefers Beatrice to Hero, but that he is against marriage. Don Pedro returns to find them and Benedick reveals that Claudio is in love with Hero.

Activity 6: Exploring Benedick's views on marriage

a. In pairs, read aloud lines 148–152, swapping readers at the punctuation marks.
b. Read lines 148–152 again as before, but this time say each new phrase as if it is a new thought.
c. Pick out the phrases from lines 148–152 that reveal Benedick's attitude to marriage.
d. In your pairs, create a **freeze-frame** in which one of you is Benedick and the other is a married man. Show exactly what Benedick's attitude is to the married man.
e. Imagining you are Benedick, write a paragraph explaining why you do not want to get married.

Glossary

149 **wear... suspicion** wear a hat to cover up his cuckold's horns
151 **yoke** a harness for a working beast
151 **Sundays** Traditional rest days when people with families had to stay at home

At the time

Using page 205, find out what a cuckold was and how he could be identified according to legend.

Did you know?

In rehearsals, actors at the RSC use the punctuation marks as an indicator of when a character's thoughts are moving from one thing to the next.

Key term

Freeze-frame a physical, still image created by people to represent an object, place, person or feeling

Claudio	In mine eye she is the sweetest lady that ever I looked on.
Benedick	I can see yet without spectacles and I see no such matter. There's her cousin, an she were not possessed with a fury, exceeds her as much in beauty as the first of May doth the last of December. But I hope you have no intent to turn husband, have you? 145
Claudio	I would scarce trust myself, though I had sworn the contrary, if Hero would be my wife.
Benedick	Is't come to this? In faith, hath not the world one man but he will wear his cap with suspicion? Shall I never see a bachelor of three-score again? Go to, i' faith and thou wilt needs thrust thy neck into a yoke, wear the print of it and sigh away Sundays. Look, Don Pedro is returned to seek you. 150

Enter Don Pedro

Don Pedro	What secret hath held you here that you followed not to Leonato's?
Benedick	I would your grace would constrain me to tell. 155
Don Pedro	I charge thee on thy allegiance.
Benedick	You hear, Count Claudio? I can be secret as a dumb man, I would have you think so – but on my allegiance, mark you this, on my allegiance – he is in love. With who? Now that is your grace's part. Mark how short his answer is: with Hero, Leonato's short daughter. 160
Claudio	If this were so, so were it uttered.
Benedick	Like the old tale, my lord: 'It is not so, nor 'twas not so, but indeed, God forbid it should be so.'
Claudio	If my passion change not shortly, God forbid it should be otherwise. 165
Don Pedro	Amen, if you love her, for the lady is very well worthy.
Claudio	You speak this to fetch me in, my lord.
Don Pedro	By my troth, I speak my thought.

Benedick gives Claudio and Don Pedro all the reasons why he will never fall in love. Don Pedro asserts that even Benedick will fall in love one day.

Don Pedro and Benedick, 2012

At the time

Using page 203, find out who Cupid was and what the conventions of courtly love were.

Activity 7: Exploring imagery

a. Read lines 167–186. Discuss the views about women and love expressed by Benedick.
b. What **imagery** does Benedick use to express his views and what does this suggest about the strength of his feelings?

Key term

Imagery visually descriptive language

Activity 8: Exploring power through movement

a. In small groups, decide who will play Don Pedro, Claudio and Benedick. Read aloud lines 167–186.
b. The people playing Don Pedro and Claudio stand rooted to the spot. They are not allowed to move from that spot. Meanwhile, the person playing Benedick moves wherever they like around the other two, experimenting with how they can use their physical presence to intimidate Don Pedro and Claudio without touching them. Read aloud lines 167–186 again, using these rules.
c. Read the lines again, but this time with Benedick rooted to the spot and the other two characters able to move wherever they like around him.
d. Discuss lines 167–186 with your group. Who is challenging whom, and when, during this section? How could you move to show that?
e. Look at the photo on this page and discuss which line you think is being spoken here. Give reasons for your suggestion.

Glossary

180–182 **I will have a recheat... invisible baldric** I will wear a hunting horn on my head or hidden on my belt. The horn is a sign of a cuckold, which is a man whose wife commits adultery

189 **ballad-maker's pen** Most ballads written were about love

194 **hang... like a cat** Sometimes cats in leather bottles were hung up for target practice

196 **Adam** Adam Bell was a famous archer at the time the play was written

Claudio	And in faith, my lord, I spoke mine.	170

Benedick And, by my two faiths and troths, my lord, I spoke mine.

Claudio That I love her, I feel.

Don Pedro That she is worthy, I know.

Benedick That I neither feel how she should be loved nor know how she
should be worthy is the opinion that fire cannot melt out of me. 175
I will die in it at the stake.

Don Pedro Thou wast ever an obstinate heretic in the despite of beauty.

Claudio And never could maintain his part but in the force of his will.

Benedick That a woman conceived me, I thank her. That she brought
me up, I likewise give her most humble thanks. But that I will 180
have a recheat winded in my forehead, or hang my bugle in an
invisible baldric, all women shall pardon me. Because I will not
do them the wrong to mistrust any, I will do myself the right to
trust none. And the fine is, for the which I may go the finer, I
will live a bachelor. 185

Don Pedro I shall see thee, ere I die, look pale with love.

Benedick With anger, with sickness, or with hunger, my lord, not with love.
Prove that ever I lose more blood with love than I will get again
with drinking, pick out mine eyes with a ballad-maker's pen
and hang me up at the door of a brothel house for the sign of 190
blind Cupid.

Don Pedro Well, if ever thou dost fall from this faith, thou wilt prove a
notable argument.

Benedick If I do, hang me in a bottle like a cat, and shoot at me, and
he that hits me, let him be clapped on the shoulder and called 195
Adam.

Don Pedro Well, as time shall try. 'In time the savage bull doth bear the yoke.'

Don Pedro sends Benedick in to accept Leonato's supper invitation. When they are alone, Claudio clarifies that Hero is Leonato's only heir and then tells Don Pedro that he desires Hero.

Glossary

204 **if Cupid... Venice** if Cupid has not used up all his arrows in Venice. Venice was thought to be the city of love

211–214 **I have... Benedick** Benedick, Claudio and Don Pedro **parody** the closing of a formal letter

216 **guarded** decorated

217 **slightly basted on** loosely attached

Did you know?

Actors use the rhythm in Shakespeare's language to help them learn their lines and understand the script. Sometimes there are irregularities in the rhythm, which can indicate a character is disturbed in some way. Sometimes characters share the rhythm, which can be a clue about how close they are or how urgent their conversation is.

Activity 9: Exploring Shakespeare's rhythm

Read the description of **iambic pentameter** in the 'Key terms' box.

a. Say out loud: 'and ONE, and TWO, and THREE, and FOUR, and FIVE'.

b. Repeat task a and clap the rhythm as you speak.

c. Read aloud lines 219–234. Try fitting the words to the iambic pentameter rhythm.

d. Put Claudio's first question at line 223 into your own words. Why do you think Claudio wants to know if Hero has a brother?

e. Clap the rhythm of line 223. Does it fit the iambic pentameter rhythm regularly?

f. Write a paragraph arguing what you think Claudio is most interested in in lines 219–234. Do you think it is the money that Hero will inherit as Leonato's heir or her beauty and personality? Give reasons for your choice.

Key terms

Parody an imitation of a style of writing, with deliberate exaggeration to make it funny

Iambic pentameter the rhythm Shakespeare uses to write his plays. Each line in this rhythm contains approximately ten **syllables**. 'Iambic' means putting the stress on the second syllable of each beat. 'Pentameter' means five beats with two syllables in each beat

Syllable part of a word that is one sound, e.g. 'highness' has two syllables – 'high' and 'ness'

Benedick	The savage bull may, but if ever the sensible Benedick bear it, pluck off the bull's horns and set them in my forehead and let me be vilely painted and in such great letters as they write 'Here is good horse to hire', let them signify under my sign 'Here you may see Benedick the married man.'

200

Claudio	If this should ever happen, thou wouldst be horn-mad.
Don Pedro	Nay, if Cupid have not spent all his quiver in Venice, thou wilt quake for this shortly.

205

Benedick	I look for an earthquake too, then.
Don Pedro	Well, you will temporize with the hours. In the meantime, good Signor Benedick, repair to Leonato's, commend me to him, and tell him I will not fail him at supper, for indeed he hath made great preparation.

210

Benedick	I have almost matter enough in me for such an embassage, and so I commit you—
Claudio	To the tuition of God. From my house if I had it—
Don Pedro	The sixth of July. Your loving friend, Benedick.

215

Benedick	Nay, mock not, mock not. The body of your discourse is sometime guarded with fragments, and the guards are but slightly basted on neither. Ere you flout old ends any further, examine your conscience. And so I leave you.

Exit Benedick

Claudio	My liege, your highness now may do me good.
Don Pedro	My love is thine to teach: teach it but how And thou shalt see how apt it is to learn Any hard lesson that may do thee good.

220

Claudio	Hath Leonato any son, my lord?
Don Pedro	No child but Hero. She's his only heir. Dost thou affect her, Claudio?
Claudio	O, my lord,

225

Don Pedro offers to **woo** Hero on Claudio's behalf.

Don Pedro and Claudio, 2012

At the time

Using pages 204–205, find out how marriages were arranged between upper-class people and what social rules there were around courtship at the time Shakespeare was writing.

Glossary

236 **book of words** love poems

238 **break with** bring it up with

244 **I would… treatise** I would have smoothed over my sudden liking by a longer explanation

246 **The fairest… necessity** the best gift is the one you want

252 **in her bosom** privately

Activity 10: Exploring status in Act 1 Scene 1

a. Go through Act 1 Scene 1 and list the characters we have met.

b. Put the list in order of richest to poorest, then most important to least important and, finally, most respected to least respected. Bear in mind whether the characters are male or female.

c. What were the differences between your lists? Status is made up of a combination of wealth, social and personal power. Which character do you think has the highest status?

d. Look at the photo on this page and decide how each character's status is suggested.

e. Consider what you have found out about **courtship** in Shakespeare's time from the 'At the time' box. Why do you think Don Pedro offers to woo Hero on Claudio's behalf?

f. Imagining you are Don Pedro, write a letter to Leonato in modern English explaining Claudio's wishes and why you have offered to woo Hero.

Key terms

Woo to try to make someone fall in love with you so that they will agree to marry you

Courtship a period of time where a couple develop a romantic relationship

When you went onward on this ended action,
I looked upon her with a soldier's eye,
That liked, but had a rougher task in hand
Than to drive liking to the name of love.
But now I am returned and that war-thoughts   230
Have left their places vacant, in their rooms
Come thronging soft and delicate desires,
All prompting me how fair young Hero is,
Saying I liked her ere I went to wars.

Don Pedro Thou wilt be like a lover presently   235
And tire the hearer with a book of words.
If thou dost love fair Hero, cherish it,
And I will break with her, and with her father,
And thou shalt have her. Was't not to this end
That thou began'st to twist so fine a story?   240

Claudio How sweetly you do minister to love,
That know love's grief by his complexion!
But lest my liking might too sudden seem
I would have salved it with a longer treatise.

Don Pedro What need the bridge much broader than the flood?   245
The fairest grant is the necessity.
Look, what will serve is fit. 'Tis once, thou lovest,
And I will fit thee with the remedy.
I know we shall have revelling tonight.
I will assume thy part in some disguise,   250
And tell fair Hero I am Claudio;
And in her bosom I'll unclasp my heart
And take her hearing prisoner with the force
And strong encounter of my amorous tale.
Then after to her father will I break,   255
And the conclusion is, she shall be thine.
In practice let us put it presently.

Exeunt

Leonato and Antonio are getting ready for the masked party they are holding that night to celebrate the safe return of Don Pedro and his men. Antonio tells Leonato that his servant has overheard Don Pedro and Claudio talking about wooing Hero, but the servant has heard wrong! Antonio thinks that Don Pedro is in love with Hero himself, so he tells Leonato that Don Pedro intends to declare his love for his daughter at the party.

Leonato and Antonio, 2006

Activity 1: Exploring language

a. In pairs, read aloud lines 1–19 with one of you as Leonato and the other as Antonio.

b. Read the lines again, but this time whisper the lines as if the characters do not want to be overheard. How does this change the scene?

c. Stand about five steps apart. Read the lines again, this time loudly. How does this change the scene?

d. Finally, read lines 1–19 again, this time varying the volume of your speech according to how you think the scene should be played.

e. Look at the photo on this page. How do you think the actors are speaking their lines? Explain your reasons.

f. Write notes on lines 1–19, describing why particular changes in volume really suited sections of the scene.

Did you know?

Actors experiment with different ways of playing a scene during rehearsals. There is no 'right' way of saying a line or of playing a particular character. Actors experiment until they find the most effective way of playing the scene in order to help the audience understand what is going on.

Act 1 | Scene 2

Enter Leonato and Antonio

Leonato How now, brother! Where is my cousin, your son? Hath he
provided this music?

Antonio He is very busy about it. But, brother, I can tell you strange news
that you yet dreamt not of.

Leonato Are they good?   5

Antonio As the event stamps them, but they have a good cover: they show
well outward. The Prince and Count Claudio, walking in a
thick-pleached alley in mine orchard, were thus much overheard
by a man of mine. The Prince discovered to Claudio that he
loved my niece, your daughter, and meant to acknowledge it this   10
night in a dance, and if he found her accordant, he meant to take
the present time by the top and instantly break with you of it.

Leonato Hath the fellow any wit that told you this?

Antonio A good sharp fellow. I will send for him, and question him
yourself.   15

Leonato No, no. We will hold it as a dream till it appear itself. But I
will acquaint my daughter withal, that she may be the better
prepared for an answer if peradventure this be true. Go you and
tell her of it.

Enter Attendants

Cousins, you know what you have to do. O, I cry you mercy,   20
friend. Go you with me, and I will use your skill. Good cousin,
have a care this busy time.

Exeunt

Activity 1: Exploring imagery

a. In pairs, read aloud Don John's speech in lines 21–29, swapping readers at the punctuation marks.

b. Read the first sentence aloud from lines 21–23 and decide which you think are the most important words. Choose at least six words.

c. Agree gestures that could go with each of the key words you have chosen. Use gestures that help you to express exactly what the character means.

d. Now read the sentence again, adding the gestures.

e. Work through the rest of the speech in the same way.

f. The imagery in Shakespeare's plays can help to give us an idea of what is on the mind of the person who is speaking. What would you say is on Don John's mind in this speech?

g. Write a paragraph that explains how the imagery Don John uses in lines 21–29 helps us to understand his character. For example, in line 21, when he describes himself as a 'canker', we could say that he sees himself as wild and diseased.

At the time

In lines 8–9, Don John talks about being 'born under Saturn'. Using page 203, explain what the Elizabethans believed about the influence of the planets on their lives.

Glossary

1 **out of measure** out of proportion
9–10 **mortifying mischief** embarrassing disgrace
13–14 **claw... humour** drag no one else into my mood
21 **a canker** a wild, diseased rose
22–23 **fashion a carriage** pretend a way of being
26 **enfranchised with a clog** set free, but with a weight on my leg

Don John, 2014

Act 1 | Scene 3

Enter Don John and Conrad

Conrad What the goodyear, my lord, why are you thus out of measure
sad?

Don John There is no measure in the occasion that breeds it, therefore the
sadness is without limit.

Conrad You should hear reason.   5

Don John And when I have heard it, what blessing brings it?

Conrad If not a present remedy, at least a patient sufferance.

Don John I wonder that thou – being, as thou say'st thou art, born under
Saturn – goest about to apply a moral medicine to a mortifying
mischief. I cannot hide what I am. I must be sad when I have   10
cause and smile at no man's jests; eat when I have stomach, and
wait for no man's leisure; sleep when I am drowsy, and tend on
no man's business; laugh when I am merry, and claw no man in
his humour.

Conrad Yea, but you must not make the full show of this till you may   15
do it without controlment. You have of late stood out against
your brother, and he hath ta'en you newly into his grace, where
it is impossible you should take true root but by the fair weather
that you make yourself. It is needful that you frame the season
for your own harvest.   20

Don John I had rather be a canker in a hedge than a rose in his grace,
and it better fits my blood to be disdained of all than to fashion
a carriage to rob love from any. In this, though I cannot be
said to be a flattering honest man, it must not be denied but
I am a plain-dealing villain. I am trusted with a muzzle and   25
enfranchised with a clog. Therefore I have decreed not to sing
in my cage. If I had my mouth, I would bite. If I had my liberty,
I would do my liking. In the meantime, let me be that I am,
and seek not to alter me.

Borachio comes in and tells Don John that Don Pedro is planning to woo Hero on Claudio's behalf.

Don John and Conrad, 2012

Activity 2: Exploring who leads whom

a. Look at the photo on this page. Who looks the most villainous in the picture? Explain your reasons.

b. In pairs, sitting on chairs, read aloud lines 31–52 with one of you as Don John and the other as Borachio.

c. Position your chairs in relation to each other according to what you think is the relationship between the characters at the beginning of this section.

d. Read lines 31–52 again, this time moving your chairs in relation to each other as the relationship between the characters develops. For example, if you think that your character is deliberately confronting the other person, you might put your chair down directly in front of them. If you think your character is sneakily giving information to the other person, you might move your chair to the side.

e. Decide at what points in lines 31–52 you think Borachio or Don John is leading the villainy. Give reasons for your suggestions.

Did you know?

Actors explore the power relationship between characters so that they can decide exactly what is going on between them. Having a solid object (like a chair) to play with can sometimes help actors to make discoveries about what is going on between the characters in a scene.

Conrad Can you make no use of your discontent? 30

Don John I make all use of it, for I use it only. Who comes here?

Enter Borachio

What news, Borachio?

Borachio I came yonder from a great supper. The Prince your brother is
royally entertained by Leonato and I can give you intelligence
of an intended marriage. 35

Don John Will it serve for any model to build mischief on? What is he for a
fool that betroths himself to unquietness?

Borachio Marry, it is your brother's right hand.

Don John Who, the most exquisite Claudio?

Borachio Even he. 40

Don John A proper squire. And who, and who? Which way looks he?

Borachio Marry, on Hero, the daughter and heir of Leonato.

Don John A very forward March chick. How came you to this?

Borachio Being entertained for a perfumer, as I was smoking a musty
room comes me the Prince and Claudio, hand in hand, in sad 45
conference. I whipped me behind the arras, and there heard it
agreed upon that the Prince should woo Hero for himself and,
having obtained her, give her to Count Claudio.

Don John Come, come, let us thither. This may prove food to my
displeasure. That young start-up hath all the glory of my 50
overthrow. If I can cross him any way I bless myself every way.
You are both sure, and will assist me?

Conrad To the death, my lord.

Don John Let us to the great supper. Their cheer is the greater that I am
subdued. Would the cook were of my mind. Shall we go prove 55
what's to be done?

Borachio We'll wait upon your lordship.

Exeunt

Benedick and Beatrice, 2006

Activity 1: Exploring the action of Act 1

In groups, look back over Act 1. Use the page summaries to prepare an entertaining short performance of the whole act.

- One person in your group reads the page summaries aloud, while the rest of the group acts out everything that happens in the most exaggerated way that they can.
- You can use single words or short lines from the text to help your performance. For example, on page 18, the page summary mentions the 'battle of wits' between Beatrice and Benedick. You might choose one or two of the things that they say on page 19 to be part of your performance.

Claudio and Benedick, 2014

Activity 2: Exploring the themes of Act 1

a. Discuss how Shakespeare develops the themes of love and marriage in Act 1 by comparing how the following characters express their ideas about these topics:
  - Benedick
  - Beatrice
  - Claudio
  - Don Pedro.

b. Write a brief essay (no more than 400 words in length) entitled: 'How does Shakespeare present the theme of love in Act 1?' You could include:
  - the ideas you have discussed in task a, including use of language and stagecraft
  - what you have noticed about the structure of Act 1
  - what you think will happen next and how Shakespeare has encouraged us to think this way.

After supper, Leonato, Antonio, Beatrice and Hero gather. They discuss what they think of Don John and then Beatrice turns the subject to Benedick. Leonato and Antonio warn Beatrice that her sharp tongue will prevent her from getting married.

At the time

Using page 204, find out how society expected unmarried women to behave in Shakespeare's time.

Beatrice, 2012

Activity 1: Exploring the relationships between characters

a. In small groups, decide who will play Leonato, Antonio, Beatrice and Hero. Read aloud lines 15–25. Hero is silent here.

b. Stand in a square, a few steps apart. To help you understand more about the characters, their relationships and their motives, read lines 15–25 again. This time, as you speak and listen, you should keep choosing between the following movements:

- Take a step towards another character.
- Take a step away from another character.
- Turn towards another character.
- Turn away from another character.
- Stand still.

Try to make instinctive choices rather than planning what to do.

c. Discuss the relationships between Leonato, Antonio, Beatrice and Hero. What ideas about the **theme** of love and marriage do they express here? What do you think Hero is thinking while the rest of her family is talking?

Glossary

8 **my lady's eldest son** i.e. a spoiled child

17 **curst** sarcastic

22 **no husband** Talk of horns leads to thoughts of cuckolding (a cuckold is a man whose wife commits adultery)

24–25 **lie in the woollen** lie between wool blankets rather than sheets

Key term

Theme the main ideas explored in a piece of literature, e.g. the themes of love and marriage, male and female relationships, deception, loyalty and honour might be considered key themes of *Much Ado About Nothing*

Act 2 | Scene 1

Enter Leonato, Antonio, Hero and Beatrice

Leonato Was not Count John here at supper?

Antonio I saw him not.

Beatrice How tartly that gentleman looks. I never can see him but I am
heartburned an hour after.

Hero He is of a very melancholy disposition. 5

Beatrice He were an excellent man that were made just in the midway
between him and Benedick: the one is too like an image
and says nothing, and the other too like my lady's eldest son,
evermore tattling.

Leonato Then half Signor Benedick's tongue in Count John's mouth, and 10
half Count John's melancholy in Signor Benedick's face.

Beatrice With a good leg and a good foot, uncle, and money enough in
his purse, such a man would win any woman in the world, if he
could get her good will.

Leonato By my troth, niece, thou wilt never get thee a husband, if thou 15
be so shrewd of thy tongue.

Antonio In faith, she's too curst.

Beatrice Too curst is more than curst. I shall lessen God's sending that
way, for it is said, 'God sends a curst cow short horns', but to a
cow too curst he sends none. 20

Leonato So, by being too curst, God will send you no horns.

Beatrice Just, if he send me no husband, for the which blessing I am at
him upon my knees every morning and evening. Lord, I could
not endure a husband with a beard on his face. I had rather lie
in the woollen. 25

Beatrice explains why she does not want a husband. Leonato advises his daughter Hero to accept Don Pedro if he proposes to her at the party, while Beatrice advises her cousin to make up her own mind about whom she wants to marry.

Antonio, Balthasar, Hero, Leonato and Beatrice, 2014

Activity 2: Exploring Hero's thoughts

a. In small groups, decide who will play Leonato, Antonio, Beatrice and Hero (who does not speak). Read aloud lines 40–52.

b. Read aloud lines 40–52 again, this time standing up. The person playing Hero should stand in the middle, with Antonio and Leonato on one side and Beatrice on the other. If the person playing Hero hears a piece of advice they like, they should take a step towards the character who has given that advice. If the person playing Hero hears a piece of advice they do not like, they should take a step away from the character who has given that advice.

c. Go back through lines 40–52 and decide what Hero is thinking at each moment. Write down those thoughts in your own words.

d. Why do you think Shakespeare put Hero in this scene, even though she hardly says anything?

Glossary

32 **in earnest of** as a down payment for

32 **the bearward** a man who kept bears and other animals for entertainment

32 **hell** Proverbially, this was the fate of unmarried women

37 **Saint Peter** the keeper of the gates of heaven

46 **mettle** material or spirit

46 **earth** According to the Bible, man was formed out of earth

49 **marl** clay

49 **Adam** the first man

55 **measure** balance and rhythm

57 **cinquepace** a dance with five steps followed by a leap

Leonato   You may light on a husband that hath no beard.

Beatrice   What should I do with him? Dress him in my apparel and make
him my waiting-gentlewoman? He that hath a beard is more
than a youth, and he that hath no beard is less than a man.
And he that is more than a youth is not for me, and he that is   30
less than a man, I am not for him. Therefore, I will even take
sixpence in earnest of the bearward and lead his apes into hell.

Leonato   Well then, go you into hell?

Beatrice   No, but to the gate, and there will the devil meet me like an old
cuckold, with horns on his head, and say, 'Get you to heaven,   35
Beatrice, get you to heaven. Here's no place for you maids.' So
deliver I up my apes and away to Saint Peter for the heavens.
He shows me where the bachelors sit, and there live we as merry
as the day is long.

Antonio   Well, niece, I trust you will be ruled by your father.   40

Beatrice   Yes, faith, it is my cousin's duty to make curtsy and say, 'Father,
as it please you.' But yet for all that, cousin, let him be a
handsome fellow, or else make another curtsy and say, 'Father, as
it please me.'

Leonato   Well, niece, I hope to see you one day fitted with a husband.   45

Beatrice   Not till God make men of some other mettle than earth.
Would it not grieve a woman to be overmastered with a
pierce of valiant dust? To make an account of her life to a clod
of wayward marl? No, uncle, I'll none. Adam's sons are my
brethren, and truly I hold it a sin to match in my kindred.   50

Leonato   Daughter, remember what I told you. If the Prince do solicit
you in that kind, you know your answer.

Beatrice   The fault will be in the music, cousin, if you be not wooed
in good time. If the Prince be too important, tell him there is
measure in everything and so dance out the answer. For, hear   55
me, Hero, wooing, wedding, and repenting is as a Scotch jig,
a measure, and a cinquepace. The first suit is hot and hasty,

The family are joined by their guests for a masked party. Disguised in their masks, Don Pedro talks of love to Hero as they dance and Balthasar dances with Margaret.

Hero and Don Pedro, 2006

Glossary

71 **favour** face
72 **case** mask
73 **Philemon** a poor man who entertained the god Jove in his cottage
74 **visor** mask

Activity 3: Exploring pronouns

a. In pairs, read aloud lines 65–74 with one of you as Don Pedro and the other as Hero. You should whisper your lines as if the characters are having a private conversation.

b. Read the lines again, this time emphasising the **pronouns** by pointing to yourself when you say 'I' or 'my' and pointing to your partner when you say 'you' or 'your'. How does this change your understanding of the scene?

c. Hero thinks Don Pedro wants to marry her. How would you describe the **tone** of this **dialogue**? How do you think Hero is feeling during lines 65–74?

d. Imagine Hero goes straight to tell her father about dancing and talking with Don Pedro (the Prince). Write the script of the conversation that Hero and Leonato might have in modern English.

At the time

Using page 202, find out about the tradition of masked parties and why masked events are included in some of Shakespeare's plays.

Key terms

Pronoun a word (such as *I*, *he*, *she*, *you*, *it*, *we* or *they*) that is used instead of a noun

Tone as in 'tone of voice'; expressing an attitude through how you say something

Dialogue a discussion between two or more people

like a Scotch jig and full as fantastical; the wedding, mannerly modest, as a measure, full of state and ancientry; and then comes repentance, and with his bad legs, falls into the cinquepace faster 60 and faster till he sink into his grave.

Leonato Cousin, you apprehend passing shrewdly.

Beatrice I have a good eye, uncle. I can see a church by daylight.

Leonato The revellers are entering, brother. Make good room.

All put on their masks. Enter, with masks, Don Pedro, Claudio, Benedick, and Balthasar, Don John, Borachio, Margaret, Ursula, musicians and servants

Don Pedro Lady, will you walk about with your friend? 65

Hero So you walk softly, and look sweetly, and say nothing, I am yours for the walk, and especially when I walk away.

Don Pedro With me in your company?

Hero I may say so when I please.

Don Pedro And when please you to say so? 70

Hero When I like your favour, for God defend the lute should be like the case.

Don Pedro My visor is Philemon's roof; within the house is Jove.

Hero Why, then, your visor should be thatched.

Don Pedro Speak low, if you speak love.

Balthasar [Drawing Margaret aside] Well, I would you did like me. 75

Margaret So would not I, for your own sake, for I have many ill qualities.

Balthasar Which is one?

Margaret I say my prayers aloud.

Balthasar I love you the better, the hearers may cry amen.

Margaret God match me with a good dancer. 80

The masked dancing continues. Hero's friend Ursula correctly guesses that she is dancing with Antonio, who makes a poor attempt to cover up who he is. Beatrice and Benedick, behind their masks, say hurtful things about each other.

Benedick and Beatrice, 2012

Activity 4: Exploring paraphrasing

a. In pairs, read aloud lines 95–106 with one of you as Beatrice and the other as Benedick.

b. Write a new script for Beatrice and Benedick, **paraphrasing** lines 95–106. Are there any bits that are difficult to paraphrase? Discuss the reasons why.

c. Remember that the characters are wearing masks. In pairs, read aloud the script you have written as if Benedick knows that he is talking to Beatrice, but she does not know who he is.

d. Read aloud your script again, this time as if Beatrice and Benedick both know who the other really is.

e. Return to Shakespeare's lines. Do you think Beatrice knows who she is dancing with during lines 95–106? Write a paragraph explaining your answer, using evidence from these lines to support your argument.

Key term

Paraphrase put a line or section of text into your own words

Did you know?

Shakespeare is very economical in his use of language, so when RSC actors are paraphrasing, they often have to use more words than Shakespeare does.

Balthasar   Amen.

Margaret   And God keep him out of my sight when the dance is done. Answer, clerk.

Balthasar   No more words, the clerk is answered.

Ursula   I know you well enough, you are Signor Antonio.   85

Antonio   At a word, I am not.

Ursula   I know you by the waggling of your head.

Antonio   To tell you true, I counterfeit him.

Ursula   You could never do him so ill-well unless you were the very man. Here's his dry hand up and down. You are he, you are he.   90

Antonio   At a word, I am not.

Ursula   Come, come, do you think I do not know you by your excellent wit? Can virtue hide itself? Go to, mum, you are he. Graces will appear, and there's an end.

Beatrice   Will you not tell me who told you so?   95

Benedick   No, you shall pardon me.

Beatrice   Nor will you not tell me who you are?

Benedick   Not now.

Beatrice   That I was disdainful, and that I had my good wit out of the Hundred Merry Tales. Well, this was Signor Benedick that   100 said so.

Benedick   What's he?

Beatrice   I am sure you know him well enough.

Benedick   Not I, believe me.

Beatrice   Did he never make you laugh?   105

Benedick   I pray you, what is he?

Beatrice   Why, he is the Prince's jester, a very dull fool. Only his gift is in

st of the company dance away, leaving Claudio, Don John and Borachio alone.
ı John pretends he thinks Claudio is Benedick and tells him that Don Pedro has sworn
ʒ in love with Hero, which is a lie. Borachio tells Claudio that Don Pedro has sworn
ıarry Hero.

John and Claudio, 2012

Activity 5: Exploring objectives and tactics

a. In small groups, decide who will play Don John, Borachio and Claudio. Read aloud lines 124–135.
b. Discuss what you think Don John and Borachio are trying to achieve in these lines. For example, Don John might want to make Claudio believe that Don Pedro loves Hero or to make Claudio hate Don Pedro. Write what you decide on a blank piece of paper. That is the character's **objective**. Place the paper and a pen in the middle of your group.
c. Now read lines 124–135 again. Every time Don John or Borachio says something that helps them to achieve their objective from task b, tick the piece of paper.
d. Look back over lines 124–135, remembering the points at which you ticked the paper. Write down on the paper the **tactics** you think Don John and Borachio used at those points.

Key terms

Objective what a character wants to get or achieve in a scene, e.g. Don John might want to make Claudio hate Don Pedro

Tactics the methods a character uses to get what they want, e.g. Don John's tactic could be to deceive

Did you know?

Actors work out what their character's objective is and what tactics they use to achieve it. This helps them communicate clearly what kind of person their character is and how they behave.

devising impossible slanders. None but libertines delight in him,
and the commendation is not in his wit but in his villainy, for
he both pleases men and angers them, and then they laugh at   110
him, and beat him. I am sure he is in the fleet. I would he had
boarded me.

Benedick When I know the gentleman, I'll tell him what you say.

Beatrice Do, do. He'll but break a comparison or two on me, which
peradventure not marked, or not laughed at, strikes him into   115
melancholy, and then there's a partridge wing saved, for the fool
will eat no supper that night. We must follow the leaders.

Benedick In every good thing.

Beatrice Nay, if they lead to any ill I will leave them at the next turning.

Music and dancing. Exeunt all but Don John, Borachio and Claudio

Don John Sure my brother is amorous on Hero and hath withdrawn her   120
father to break with him about it. The ladies follow her and but
one visor remains.

Borachio And that is Claudio. I know him by his bearing.

Don John Are not you Signor Benedick?

Claudio You know me well, I am he.   125

Don John Signor, you are very near my brother in his love. He is
enamoured on Hero. I pray you, dissuade him from her. She is
no equal for his birth. You may do the part of an honest man
in it.

Claudio How know you he loves her?   130

Don John I heard him swear his affection.

Borachio So did I too, and he swore he would marry her tonight.

Don John Come, let us to the banquet.

Exeunt all but Claudio

Claudio Thus answer I in the name of Benedick,

Claudio, misled by Don John, thinks Don Pedro is in love with Hero. Benedick comes in and asks Claudio what he is going to do about it. Claudio says very little and leaves. Left alone, Benedick's thoughts turn to what Beatrice has said to him during the masked dancing.

Benedick and Claudio, 2012

Activity 6: Exploring the theme of loyalty

a. In pairs, read aloud lines 145–159 with one of you as Benedick and the other as Claudio.

b. Who speaks the most during these lines? Why do you think Claudio says so little? What ideas are expressed about the theme of loyalty?

c. Go through lines 145–159 and choose ten words in total. Make sure you choose powerful words that are absolutely essential to understanding the conversation between Benedick and Claudio. Include words for both characters. For example, from line 147 you might choose 'come' or 'go'.

d. In character, read aloud the powerful words you have chosen to your partner, and then stand up and create **gestures** to go with each word you have chosen. Look at the photo and think about what word might be spoken here.

e. Imagining you are Claudio, write a letter to Don Pedro in modern English explaining how you feel and why.

Glossary

139 **all hearts... tongues** all those in love speak for themselves

142 **faith** loyalty

142 **blood** desire

143 **an accident... proof** something that happens all the time

144 **mistrusted not** did not suspect

149 **willow** The willow tree was an emblem of unrequited love

149–150 **What fashion... garland of** how will you wear the dishonour that the Prince has done you

151 **usurer** moneylender

151 **lieutenant's scarf** soldier's sash

154 **drover** cattle dealer

157–158 **strike... post** Benedick refers to a story about a servant who tricks his blind master into hitting a post

160 **sedges** plants like grass that grow in cold, wet places

Key term

Gesture a movement, often using the hands or head, to express a feeling or idea

But hear these ill news with the ears of Claudio.   135
'Tis certain so, the Prince woos for himself.
Friendship is constant in all other things
Save in the office and affairs of love.
Therefore all hearts in love use their own tongues.
Let every eye negotiate for itself,   140
And trust no agent, for beauty is a witch
Against whose charms faith melteth into blood.
This is an accident of hourly proof,
Which I mistrusted not. Farewell, therefore, Hero.

Enter Benedick

Benedick Count Claudio?   145

Claudio Yea, the same.

Benedick Come, will you go with me?

Claudio Whither?

Benedick Even to the next willow, about your own business, County. What
fashion will you wear the garland of? About your neck, like an   150
usurer's chain? Or under your arm, like a lieutenant's scarf?
You must wear it one way, for the Prince hath got your Hero.

Claudio I wish him joy of her.

Benedick Why, that's spoken like an honest drover, so they sell bullocks.
But did you think the Prince would have served you thus?   155

Claudio I pray you, leave me.

Benedick Ho, now you strike like the blind man: 'twas the boy that stole
your meat, and you'll beat the post.

Claudio If it will not be, I'll leave you.

Exit Claudio

Benedick Alas, poor hurt fowl, now will he creep into sedges. But that my   160
Lady Beatrice should know me, and not know me! The Prince's
fool! Ha? It may be I go under that title because I am merry.
Yea, but so I am apt to do myself wrong. I am not so reputed.

Don Pedro comes looking for Count Claudio. He finds Benedick, who challenges him for stealing Hero from Claudio. Don Pedro tells Benedick that Beatrice is angry with him. Benedick tells the Prince (Don Pedro) what he thinks of Beatrice.

Activity 7: Exploring what one character says about another

a. In pairs, read aloud lines 194–205, swapping readers at the end of each sentence.

b. Write a list of all the things that Benedick says about Beatrice in lines 194–205.

c. In your own words, write down characteristics that sum up each of the things on your list from task b. For example, when Benedick says 'If her breath were as terrible as her terminations, there were no living near her', you could write 'abusive and disgusting'.

d. With one of you as Beatrice and the other as Benedick, work together to create a sequence of **statues** that show each characteristic of Beatrice as Benedick sees her. The person playing Benedick should read lines 194–205, while the person playing Beatrice moves through their sequence of statues.

e. Write a paragraph that explains which of the statues was the most effective and why. Think about how the characteristics shown help you to understand the theme of male and female relationships in the play.

Benedick, 2014

Glossary

164–165 **puts... person** thinks everybody thinks like her
165 **gives me out** talks about me
168 **Lady Fame** rumour
169 **as melancholy... warren** sad and lonely, like a gamekeeper's hut in the middle of nowhere
175 **flat** undeniable
192 **great thaw** huge snowfall melting, perhaps dull because everyone has to stay in
193 **impossible conveyance** incredible skill
194 **poniards** daggers

Key term

Statue like a freeze-frame but usually of a single character

It is the base, though bitter, disposition of Beatrice that puts the
world into her person, and so gives me out. Well, I'll be revenged   165
as I may.

Enter Don Pedro

Don Pedro   Now, Signor, where's the Count? Did you see him?

Benedick   Troth, my lord, I have played the part of Lady Fame. I found
him here as melancholy as a lodge in a warren. I told him, and
I think I told him true, that your grace had got the good will of   170
this young lady and I offered him my company to a willow-tree,
either to make him a garland, as being forsaken, or to bind him
up a rod, as being worthy to be whipped.

Don Pedro   To be whipped? What's his fault?

Benedick   The flat transgression of a schoolboy who, being overjoyed with   175
finding a bird's nest, shows it his companion, and he steals it.

Don Pedro   Wilt thou make a trust a transgression? The transgression is in
the stealer.

Benedick   Yet it had not been amiss the rod had been made, and the
garland too, for the garland he might have worn himself, and   180
the rod he might have bestowed on you, who, as I take it, have
stolen his bird's nest.

Don Pedro   I will but teach them to sing, and restore them to the owner.

Benedick   If their singing answer your saying, by my faith, you say
honestly.   185

Don Pedro   The Lady Beatrice hath a quarrel to you. The gentleman that
danced with her told her she is much wronged by you.

Benedick   O, she misused me past the endurance of a block. An oak but
with one green leaf on it would have answered her. My very
visor began to assume life and scold with her. She told me, not   190
thinking I had been myself, that I was the Prince's jester, that I
was duller than a great thaw, huddling jest upon jest with such
impossible conveyance upon me that I stood like a man at a
mark with a whole army shooting at me. She speaks poniards

Beatrice comes in with Claudio, Leonato and Hero. Benedick asks Don Pedro to send him on an errand so that he can avoid Beatrice and then leaves. Beatrice hints that she has had a relationship with Benedick in the past.

Beatrice and Benedick, 2014

Key terms

Backstory what happened to any of the characters before the start of the play

Motivation a person's reason for doing something

Did you know?

Actors use the clues in the text to work out the **backstory** of what might have happened between the characters before the play starts. Agreeing what the backstory could be means that the actors have a shared understanding of the characters' **motivations** during the play.

Activity 8: Exploring backstory

a. In groups, look at lines 217–221 in which Beatrice mentions her relationship with Benedick before the play starts.

b. Discuss why you think Beatrice says that she gave Benedick 'a double heart for his single one' and that he won her heart with 'false dice'.

c. Using the clues in lines 217–221, decide what you think the backstory between them is. Look back at Act 1 Scene 1 line 109 when Beatrice says to Benedick, 'You always end with a jade's trick. I know you of old.' How might this line add to our understanding of their backstory?

d. Imagining you are Beatrice, write the backstory from her point of view.

Glossary

196 **terminations** ends of sentences

198 **all... transgressed** In the Bible, Adam was the first man on earth and owned the whole world before he sinned

199 **Hercules** demigod of strength (in Roman mythology)

199 **turned spit** turn the handle to roast meat, like a kitchen servant

201 **Ate** the Greek goddess of mischief

202 **conjure her** cast the Devil out of her

208 **the Antipodes** the opposite side of the world

210–211 **Prester John** a legendary African or Asian king

211 **Great Cham** Kubla Khan, ruler of Tartary

213 **harpy** mythological bird of prey with the face of a woman

and every word stabs. If her breath were as terrible as her   195
terminations, there were no living near her; she would infect
to the North Star. I would not marry her though she were
endowed with all that Adam had left him before he transgressed.
She would have made Hercules have turned spit, yea, and have
cleft his club to make the fire, too. Come, talk not of her, you   200
shall find her the infernal Ate in good apparel. I would to God
some scholar would conjure her, for certainly, while she is here,
a man may live as quiet in hell as in a sanctuary, and people
sin upon purpose because they would go thither; so, indeed all
disquiet, horror, and perturbation follows her.   205

Enter Claudio, Beatrice, Leonato and Hero

Don Pedro Look, here she comes.

Benedick Will your grace command me any service to the world's end?
I will go on the slightest errand now to the Antipodes that you
can devise to send me on. I will fetch you a tooth-picker now
from the furthest inch of Asia; bring you the length of Prester   210
John's foot; fetch you a hair off the Great Cham's beard; do you
any embassage to the Pygmies, rather than hold three words'
conference with this harpy. You have no employment for me?

Don Pedro None but to desire your good company.

Benedick O God, sir, here's a dish I love not. I cannot endure my Lady   215
Tongue.

Exit Benedick

Don Pedro Come, lady, come, you have lost the heart of Signor Benedick.

Beatrice Indeed, my lord, he lent it me a while, and I gave him use for it,
a double heart for his single one. Marry, once before he won it
of me with false dice; therefore your grace may well say I have   220
lost it.

Don Pedro You have put him down, lady, you have put him down.

Don Pedro cheers Claudio up with the news that Hero has agreed to marry the Count. Leonato gives his formal permission for the engagement. Beatrice says she is unlikely to get a husband and Don Pedro offers her his hand in marriage.

Don Pedro and Beatrice, 2012

Activity 9: Exploring interpretations

a. In pairs, read aloud lines 250–264 with one of you as Beatrice and the other as Don Pedro. Experiment with the following interpretations:
   i. Read the lines as if the characters do not mean what they say.
   ii. Read the lines as if Don Pedro really does want to marry Beatrice, but she is not interested.
   iii. Read the lines as if they are both lonely and want to get married, but this is the first time that either of them has ever thought about the other as a possibility.

b. Agree what your version of the lines will be.

c. Join up with another pair and read through your agreed version of the lines. Discuss the differences between your versions of the scene.

d. Look at the photo on this page. Which interpretation do you think this photo shows? Give reasons for your suggestion.

e. Write a series of directions for two actors playing lines 250–264.

Glossary

231 **civil as an orange** This is a **pun** on Seville oranges, which are yellow, the colour of jealousy

234 **conceit** understanding

235 **broke with** broached the subject with

238–239 **Count, take of me... amen to it** Leonato uses formal language, which makes the engagement official and binding

247–248 **on the windy side of care** upwind of trouble

251 **sunburnt** It was undesirable to be suntanned in Elizabethan England

Key term

Pun a play on words

Beatrice So I would not he should do me, my lord, lest I should prove the
mother of fools. I have brought Count Claudio, whom you sent
me to seek.   225

Don Pedro Why, how now, Count, wherefore are you sad?

Claudio Not sad, my lord.

Don Pedro How then? Sick?

Claudio Neither, my lord.

Beatrice The Count is neither sad, nor sick, nor merry, nor well, but   230
civil count, civil as an orange, and something of that jealous
complexion.

Don Pedro I' faith, lady, I think your blazon to be true, though, I'll be
sworn, if he be so, his conceit is false. Here, Claudio, I have
wooed in thy name, and fair Hero is won. I have broke with her   235
father, and his good will obtained. Name the day of marriage,
and God give thee joy.

Leonato Count, take of me my daughter, and with her my fortunes. His
grace hath made the match, and all grace say amen to it.

Beatrice Speak, Count, 'tis your cue.   240

Claudio Silence is the perfectest herald of joy. I were but little happy, if I
could say how much. Lady, as you are mine, I am yours. I give
away myself for you, and dote upon the exchange.

Beatrice Speak, cousin. Or, if you cannot, stop his mouth with a kiss, and
let not him speak, neither.   245

Don Pedro In faith, lady, you have a merry heart.

Beatrice Yea, my lord, I thank it. Poor fool, it keeps on the windy side of
care. My cousin tells him in his ear that he is in her heart.

Claudio And so she doth, cousin.

Beatrice Good Lord, for alliance. Thus goes everyone to the world but I,   250
and I am sunburnt. I may sit in a corner and cry 'Heigh-ho for
a husband'.

nato sends Beatrice out to do some household duties. The date for Claudio
[ding is set for one week's time and Don Pedro suggests that during that tim
te Beatrice and Benedick fall in love with each other.

At the time

Using page ї
what the Eliz
believed abc
elements th
human bein

Benedick and

Activity 10: Exploring points of view on Beatrice and Benedick

a. Look carefully at the photo on this page of Beatrice dancing with Benedick
in his mask, from the 2006 RSC production. How would you describe each
character from what you can see in the photo? How would you describe
the relationship between them?

b. Look back over the events of Act 2 Scene 1. From what you have explored,
why would you say the designer of the 2006 RSC production chose a
monkey mask for Benedick?

c. In pairs, read aloud lines 272–276 with one of you as Don Pedro and the
other as Leonato. Why do you think Don Pedro says that Beatrice would be
an excellent wife for Benedick?

d. In the role of the same character, write a letter advising Beatrice who she
should marry and why.

e. Swap letters with your partner and discuss any differences in the advice
offered. Why do you think Shakespeare includes characters with different
viewpoints on the theme of marriage in this play?

Don Pedro Lady Beatrice, I will get you one.

Beatrice I would rather have one of your father's getting. Hath your
grace ne'er a brother like you? Your father got excellent   255
husbands, if a maid could come by them.

Don Pedro Will you have me, Lady?

Beatrice No, my lord, unless I might have another for working days. Your
grace is too costly to wear every day. But, I beseech your grace,
pardon me. I was born to speak all mirth and no matter.   260

Don Pedro Your silence most offends me, and to be merry best becomes you.
For, out of question, you were born in a merry hour.

Beatrice No, sure, my lord, my mother cried. But then there was a star
danced, and under that was I born. Cousins, God give you joy.

Leonato Niece, will you look to those things I told you of?   265

Beatrice I cry you mercy, uncle. By your grace's pardon.

Exit Beatrice

Don Pedro By my troth, a pleasant-spirited lady.

Leonato There's little of the melancholy element in her, my lord. She is
never sad but when she sleeps, and not ever sad then, for I have
heard my daughter say she hath often dreamed of unhappiness   270
and waked herself with laughing.

Don Pedro She cannot endure to hear tell of a husband.

Leonato O, by no means. She mocks all her wooers out of suit.

Don Pedro She were an excellent wife for Benedick.

Leonato O Lord, my lord, if they were but a week married, they would   275
talk themselves mad.

Don Pedro Count Claudio, when mean you to go to church?

Claudio Tomorrow, my lord. Time goes on crutches till love have all
his rites.

Leonato, Claudio and Hero agree to help Don Pedro with his plan to make Beatrice and Benedick fall in love with each other within the week.

Ursula, Antonio, Benedick, Leonato, Margaret, Don Pedro, Beatrice, Claudio and servants, 2014

Did you know?

Actors try to play every moment of the play as if it is the first time it has happened and as if anything could happen next, in order to keep the action believable.

Activity 11: Predicting the plot

a. In groups, read aloud Don Pedro's speech from lines 294–302, swapping readers at the punctuation marks.

b. Work out in detail what you think Don Pedro's plan might be. Look back over Act 2 Scene 1 and make sure you are using all the clues from the scene.

c. Write a speech for Don Pedro in modern English in which he explains his plan to Leonato, Claudio and Hero.

d. In your group, one person should read the speech you have written for Don Pedro as if they are that character. The rest of the group should act out the plan, playing the other characters that Don Pedro mentions, as required. The action should be exaggerated and clear, in the style of a silent film.

Glossary

281 **answer my mind** as I want them

284 **Hercules' labours** The demigod of strength completed 12 nearly impossible tasks (in mythology)

286 **fain** like to

295 **strain** blood

295–296 **approved valour** bravery proved in battle

Leonato   Not till Monday, my dear son, which is hence a just seven-night,   280
and a time too brief, too, to have all things answer my mind.

Don Pedro   Come, you shake the head at so long a breathing, but I warrant
thee, Claudio, the time shall not go dully by us. I will in the
interim undertake one of Hercules' labours, which is, to bring
Signor Benedick and the Lady Beatrice into a mountain of   285
affection th'one with th'other. I would fain have it a match, and
I doubt not but to fashion it, if you three will but minister such
assistance as I shall give you direction.

Leonato   My lord, I am for you, though it cost me ten nights' watchings.

Claudio   And I, my lord.   290

Don Pedro   And you too, gentle Hero?

Hero   I will do any modest office, my lord, to help my cousin to a
good husband.

Don Pedro   And Benedick is not the unhopefullest husband that I know.
Thus far can I praise him: he is of a noble strain, of approved   295
valour and confirmed honesty. I will teach you how to humour
your cousin, that she shall fall in love with Benedick, and I, with
your two helps, will so practise on Benedick that, in despite of
his quick wit and his queasy stomach, he shall fall in love with
Beatrice. If we can do this, Cupid is no longer an archer, his   300
glory shall be ours, for we are the only love-gods. Go in with
me, and I will tell you my drift.

Exeunt

Borachio proposes a plan to Don John that will ruin Don Pedro's plans for Claudio and Hero. He suggests that they make Claudio and Don Pedro believe that Hero is having an affair with another man.

Glossary
16 **temper** concoct
18 **estimation** merit
19 **stale** prostitute
24 **Only** for no other reason but
25 **meet** appropriate

Key term
Freeze-frame a physical, still image created by people to represent an object, place, person or feeling

Activity 1: Exploring the theme of deception

a. In pairs, read aloud lines 9–38 with one of you as Don John and other as Borachio.
b. Join up with another pair and discuss what the plan is that Borachio proposes.
c. Write down the plan as a sequence of events.
d. Create a **freeze-frame** for each of the events in the plan.
e. Choose a line from lines 9–38 to go with each of your freeze-frames. Think about what line might go with the photo on this page and why.
f. Share your version with the rest of the class.
g. Write a paragraph that explains how Borachio's plan helps to develop the theme of deception.

At the time
There is no specific reference to Don John being illegitimate until Benedick mentions it in Act 4 Scene 1. Using page 205, explain the difference Don John's illegitimacy would make to the Elizabethan audience and how they would know he was illegitimate if it is not mentioned until Act 4.

Act 2 | Scene 2

Enter Don John and Borachio

Don John   It is so. The Count Claudio shall marry the daughter of Leonato.

Borachio   Yea, my lord, but I can cross it.

Don John   Any bar, any cross, any impediment will be medicinable to me.
I am sick in displeasure to him, and whatsoever comes athwart
his affection ranges evenly with mine. How canst thou cross this   5
marriage?

Borachio   Not honestly, my lord, but so covertly that no dishonesty shall
appear in me.

Don John   Show me briefly how.

Borachio   I think I told your lordship a year since how much I am in the   10
favour of Margaret, the waiting gentlewoman to Hero.

Don John   I remember.

Borachio   I can, at any unseasonable instant of the night appoint her to
look out at her lady's chamber window.

Don John   What life is in that to be the death of this marriage?   15

Borachio   The poison of that lies in you to temper. Go you to the Prince
your brother. Spare not to tell him that he hath wronged his
honour in marrying the renowned Claudio – whose estimation
do you mightily hold up – to a contaminated stale, such a one
as Hero.   20

Don John   What proof shall I make of that?

Borachio   Proof enough to misuse the Prince, to vex Claudio, to undo
Hero and kill Leonato. Look you for any other issue?

Don John   Only to despite them, I will endeavour anything.

Borachio   Go then. Find me a meet hour to draw Don Pedro and the   25

Borachio suggests that he persuades Margaret, Hero's lady-in-waiting, to pretend to be Hero while he pretends to be Claudio at Hero's bedroom window. He proposes that Don John bring Don Pedro and Claudio to see this the night before the wedding so that they think they are seeing Hero having an affair with another man. Don John agrees and promises to pay Borachio a thousand ducats.

Borachio and Don John, 2006

Activity 2: Exploring character motivation

a. In pairs, read aloud the whole of Act 2 Scene 2 with one of you as Don John and the other as Borachio.

b. Read the lines again, but this time listen carefully to your partner and, before you read your lines, repeat out loud a significant phrase that you have heard the previous speaker say. Use what you have heard to help you to deliver your own lines more convincingly.

c. Discuss which character you think is in charge in this scene. Who has all the ideas? Why do you think Don John decides to pay Borachio a thousand gold coins if the plan succeeds?

d. Imagine you are Don John. Write a diary entry in modern English, explaining what you think of Borachio and his plan, what your hopes and fears are, and why you have offered to pay Borachio a thousand gold coins. Include a few quotations from Act 2 Scene 2 in the diary entry.

Glossary

27 **Intend** pretend
29 **cozened** cheated
30 **semblance** appearance
38 **assurance** proof
40 **ducats** gold coins

Did you know?

Actors listen carefully when they are exploring a scene to make sure they are using all the evidence in the text.

Count Claudio alone. Tell them that you know that Hero loves me. Intend a kind of zeal both to the Prince and Claudio – as in love of your brother's honour who hath made this match, and his friend's reputation, who is thus like to be cozened with the semblance of a maid – that you have discovered thus. They will scarcely believe this without trial. Offer them instances which shall bear no less likelihood than to see me at her chamber window, hear me call Margaret Hero, hear Margaret term me Claudio. And bring them to see this the very night before the intended wedding. For in the meantime I will so fashion the matter that Hero shall be absent, and there shall appear such seeming truth of Hero's disloyalty that jealousy shall be called assurance and all the preparation overthrown.

Don John Grow this to what adverse issue it can, I will put it in practice. Be cunning in the working this and thy fee is a thousand ducats.

Borachio Be you constant in the accusation and my cunning shall not shame me.

Don John I will presently go learn their day of marriage.

Exeunt

Benedick is in the orchard of Leonato's home. He sends a servant to get a book for him from his room. Left alone, he shares his thoughts and feelings about Claudio being in love and speculates about what his ideal woman would be like.

Benedick, 2014

Activity 1: Exploring the theme of male and female relationships

a. In pairs, read aloud lines 11–19, swapping readers at the punctuation marks.

b. Read lines 11–19 again, swapping readers at the punctuation marks. This time, try hard to convince your partner that what you are saying is true and that it is the most important thing being said.

c. Read the lines again, this time physically showing your partner what Claudio is like as you speak. For example, in lines 13–15, one of you will show Claudio being manly and interested in wearing armour and then the other will show Claudio fussing over wearing a fashionable outfit.

d. In the same pairs, read aloud lines 22–30 in the same way: swapping readers at the punctuation marks, convincing each other of what you are saying and showing each other what the woman you are describing is like as you speak. For example, in line 23, when you say 'another is wise' you might point to your head, showing us that she is good at using her brain.

e. Draw or write notes on the ideal woman as Benedick sees her. Use the words that Benedick uses to describe his ideal woman in lines 22–30 in your notes or to decorate your drawing.

Did you know?

When an actor is delivering a **soliloquy**, they will often talk to the audience as if they are another character in the play – someone who can help them find the answers to their dilemma or problem. This helps them to build a direct relationship with the audience.

Key term

Soliloquy a speech in which a character is alone on stage and expresses their thoughts and feelings aloud to the audience

Act 2 | Scene 3

Enter Benedick

Benedick Boy!

Enter Boy

Boy Signor?

Benedick In my chamber-window lies a book. Bring it hither to me in the orchard.

Boy I am here already, sir.   5

Benedick I know that, but I would have thee hence and here again.

Exit Boy

I do much wonder that one man, seeing how much another man is a fool when he dedicates his behaviours to love, will, after he hath laughed at such shallow follies in others, become the argument of his own scorn by falling in love; and such a   10 man is Claudio. I have known when there was no music with him but the drum and the fife, and now had he rather hear the tabor and the pipe. I have known when he would have walked ten mile afoot to see a good armour, and now will he lie ten nights awake carving the fashion of a new doublet. He was   15 wont to speak plain and to the purpose, like an honest man and a soldier, and now is he turned orthography. His words are a very fantastical banquet, just so many strange dishes. May I be so converted and see with these eyes? I cannot tell. I think not. I will not be sworn, but love may transform me to an oyster, but   20 I'll take my oath on it, till he have made an oyster of me, he shall never make me such a fool. One woman is fair, yet I am well; another is wise, yet I am well; another virtuous, yet I am well. But till all graces be in one woman, one woman shall not come in my grace. Rich she shall be, that's certain; wise, or I'll   25 none; virtuous, or I'll never cheapen her; fair, or I'll never look

Don Pedro, Leonato and Claudio gather to listen to music made by Balthasar, Don Pedro's servant. When they arrive, Benedick hides himself 'in the arbour', but Don Pedro spots where he is hiding.

Clockwise from the top: Benedick and Balthasar, 2014; Balthasar, 2012; Balthasar, 2006

Glossary

27 **noble** of high social status or a coin
27 **angel** a coin
30 **arbour** a place sheltered by trees or plants
50 **crotchets** quarter notes in music
51 **nothing** nothing else
53 **sheeps' guts** strings on instruments
53 **hale** draw
53 **horn** hunting horn

Activity 2: Exploring how music makes meaning on stage

a. In pairs, read aloud lines 31–33 and lines 37–48. From these lines, pick out any clues in the script about the atmosphere and mood of the evening.

b. Look at the photos on this page, which show this moment in the play from three different RSC productions: the 2006 production (bottom left) was set in 1950s Cuba, the 2012 production (right) was set in modern India and the 2014 production (top left) was set in England just after the First World War. Using the photos as inspiration, imagine the music that might go with each one.

c. Write down five words inspired by each photo that could be used to describe the atmosphere and mood of each production.

on her; mild, or come not near me; noble, or not I for an angel;
of good discourse; an excellent musician; and her hair shall be of
what colour it please God. Ha! The Prince and Monsieur Love.
I will hide me in the arbour.   30

Enter Don Pedro, Leonato, Claudio and Balthasar

Don Pedro Come, shall we hear this music?

Claudio Yea, my good lord. How still the evening is,
As hushed on purpose to grace harmony.

Don Pedro [Aside] See you where Benedick hath hid himself?

Claudio [Aside] O very well, my lord. The music ended,   35
We'll fit the kid-fox with a pennyworth.

Don Pedro Come, Balthasar, we'll hear that song again.

Balthasar O good my lord, tax not so bad a voice
To slander music any more than once.

Don Pedro It is the witness still of excellency   40
To put a strange face on his own perfection.
I pray thee sing, and let me woo no more.

Balthasar Because you talk of wooing I will sing.
Since many a wooer doth commence his suit
To her he thinks not worthy, yet he woos,   45
Yet will he swear he loves.

Don Pedro   Nay, pray thee, come.
Or if thou wilt hold longer argument,
Do it in notes.

Balthasar   Note this before my notes.
There's not a note of mine that's worth the noting.

Don Pedro Why, these are very crotchets that he speaks,   50
Note notes, forsooth, and nothing.

Benedick Now, divine air! Now is his soul ravished. Is it not strange that
sheeps' guts should hale souls out of men's bodies? Well, a horn
for my money, when all's done.

Balthasar sings his song and is congratulated by Don Pedro. Don Pedro starts a conversation with Claudio and Leonato about Beatrice being in love with Benedick, which Benedick overhears.

Benedick, 2014

Glossary

64 **dumps** sad tunes
76 **as lief** rather
76 **night-raven** bird of bad luck

Activity 3: Exploring performance through design

a. Look at the photos on this page of the arbour where Benedick hides. For each photo, write designer's notes on what you can see. Be as detailed as you can, describing the colours and textures, as well as the things in the photos.

b. For each photo, add your thoughts on the following questions to your notes:

   i. What would happen if Benedick was to move suddenly in his hiding place?

   ii. How would the 'arbour' move?

   iii. What sounds would the audience be able to hear?

   iv. Would it be comfortable for Benedick or not?

Benedick, 2006

Balthasar	[Sings] Sigh no more, ladies, sigh no more,	55

Balthasar [Sings] Sigh no more, ladies, sigh no more,   55
 Men were deceivers ever,
 One foot in sea and one on shore,
 To one thing constant never.
 Then sigh not so, but let them go,
 And be you blithe anwd bonny,   60
 Converting all your sounds of woe
 Into hey nonny, nonny.

 Sing no more ditties, sing no more,
 Of dumps so dull and heavy.
 The fraud of men was ever so,   65
 Since summer first was leafy.
 Then sigh not so, but let them go,
 And be you blithe and bonny,
 Converting all your sounds of woe
 Into hey nonny, nonny   70

Don Pedro By my troth, a good song.

Balthasar And an ill singer, my lord.

Don Pedro Ha, no, no, faith. Thou sing'st well enough for a shift.

Benedick And he had been a dog that should have howled thus, they would have hanged him, and I pray God his bad voice bode no   75 mischief. I had as lief have heard the night-raven, come what plague could have come after it.

Don Pedro Yea, marry, dost thou hear, Balthasar? I pray thee get us some excellent music, for tomorrow night we would have it at the Lady Hero's chamber-window.   80

Balthasar The best I can, my lord.

Don Pedro Do so. Farewell.

Exit Balthasar

Come hither, Leonato. What was it you told me of today, that your niece Beatrice was in love with Signor Benedick?

Don Pedro, Leonato and Claudio pretend that Beatrice has told them that she is in love with Benedick and that Hero has witnessed Beatrice passionately writing letters to Benedick in the middle of the night.

Claudio, Leonato and Don Pedro, 2006

Activity 4: Exploring staging

a. In small groups, decide who will play Don Pedro, Leonato, Claudio and Benedick. Read aloud lines 83–117.

b. Discuss and agree where in Leonato's house or garden this scene might take place. Use chairs to mark where things like bushes or paths might be.

c. Position yourselves so that the person playing Benedick is hiding and the other three characters are where he can overhear them.

d. Now read aloud lines 83–117 again in the stage space you have marked. This time, experiment with volume so that it is very clear who can hear what. Stop and discuss lines that you are not sure about until you agree who should hear them.

e. Join with another group and share your work with each other. Make sure that any lines that you think a character speaks to the audience are spoken directly to them.

f. Imagine you are the **director** of lines 83–117. Write director's notes describing how you think these lines should be staged and why.

Glossary

85 **stalk on** hunt

85 **the fowl sits** He is like a sitting duck

90 **Sits... corner** is that how things are

106 **gull** trick

Key term

Director the person who enables the practical and creative interpretation of a dramatic script, and ultimately brings together everybody's ideas in a way that engages the audience with the play

Claudio	[Aside] O, ay, stalk on, stalk on – the fowl sits.	85
	[Aloud] I did never think that lady would have loved any man.	
Leonato	No, nor I neither. But most wonderful that she should so dote on Signor Benedick, whom she hath in all outward behaviours seemed ever to abhor.	
Benedick	Is't possible? Sits the wind in that corner?	90
Leonato	By my troth, my lord, I cannot tell what to think of it. But that she loves him with an enraged affection, it is past the infinite of thought.	
Don Pedro	Maybe she doth but counterfeit.	
Claudio	Faith, like enough.	95
Leonato	O God! Counterfeit? There was never counterfeit of passion came so near the life of passion as she discovers it.	
Don Pedro	Why, what effects of passion shows she?	
Claudio	[Aside] Bait the hook well. This fish will bite.	
Leonato	What effects, my lord? She will sit you – you heard my daughter tell you how.	100
Claudio	She did indeed.	
Don Pedro	How, how, I pray you? You amaze me. I would have thought her spirit had been invincible against all assaults of affection.	
Leonato	I would have sworn it had, my lord, especially against Benedick.	105
Benedick	I should think this a gull, but that the white-bearded fellow speaks it. Knavery cannot, sure, hide himself in such reverence.	
Claudio	[Aside] He hath ta'en th'infection. Hold it up.	
Don Pedro	Hath she made her affection known to Benedick?	
Leonato	No, and swears she never will. That's her torment.	110
Claudio	'Tis true, indeed, so your daughter says. 'Shall I,' says she, 'that have so oft encountered him with scorn, write to him that I love him?'	

Leonato, Claudio and Don Pedro continue to trick Benedick, adding further detail to their lies about Beatrice's supposed desperate behaviour.

Claudio, Don Pedro and Leonato, 2012

Activity 5: Exploring the theme of deception

a. In pairs, read aloud lines 118–133 with one of you as Leonato and the other as Claudio.

b. The offstage events described here are made up by Leonato and Claudio to fool Benedick. Imagine the scene that they describe by picking out everything that Leonato and Claudio describe Beatrice and Hero doing.

c. Write the script of this imagined scene in modern English, using no more than ten lines. Use the detail from lines 118–133 in your script. Use as few **stage directions** as possible, instead making the action of the scene as clear as you can through what Beatrice and Hero say to each other.

d. Join up with another pair, swap your scenes and act them out for each other on your feet. Discuss anything that is challenging to understand, say or do.

e. Redraft your scenes in response to this feedback.

Glossary

121 **between the sheet** in the letter or in bed sheets (an old joke)

138 **alms** act of charity

142 **blood** passion

Key term

Stage direction an instruction in the text of a play, e.g. indicating which characters enter and exit a scene

Leonato   This says she now when she is beginning to write to him, for she'll be up twenty times a night, and there will she sit in her smock till she have writ a sheet of paper. My daughter tells us all. 115

Claudio   Now you talk of a sheet of paper, I remember a pretty jest your daughter told us of.

Leonato   O, when she had writ it and was reading it over, she found Benedick and Beatrice between the sheet. 120

Claudio   That.

Leonato   O, she tore the letter into a thousand halfpence, railed at herself, that she should be so immodest to write to one that she knew would flout her. 'I measure him,' says she, 'by my own spirit, for I should flout him if he writ to me, yea, though I love him, I should.' 125

Claudio   Then down upon her knees she falls, weeps, sobs, beats her heart, tears her hair, prays, curses: 'O sweet Benedick, God give me patience.' 130

Leonato   She doth indeed, my daughter says so, and the ecstasy hath so much overborne her that my daughter is sometime afeard she will do a desperate outrage to herself. It is very true.

Don Pedro   It were good that Benedick knew of it by some other, if she will not discover it. 135

Claudio   To what end? He would make but a sport of it and torment the poor lady worse.

Don Pedro   And he should, it were an alms to hang him. She's an excellent sweet lady, and, out of all suspicion, she is virtuous.

Claudio   And she is exceeding wise. 140

Don Pedro   In everything but in loving Benedick.

Leonato   O my lord, wisdom and blood combating in so tender a body, we have ten proofs to one that blood hath the victory. I am sorry for her, as I have just cause, being her uncle and her guardian. 145

Claudio, Don Pedro and Leonato continue their trick. Aware that Benedick can hear them, they take the opportunity to describe him in detail and then say that they won't tell Benedick about Beatrice's supposed feelings for him.

Don Pedro, Leonato and Claudio, 2014

Activity 6: Exploring language and character

a. In small groups, decide who will play Don Pedro, Claudio and Benedick (who is silent). Read aloud lines 154–161.

b. Pick out all the things that the other characters say about Benedick. Paraphrase each one by writing it in your own words. For example, in line 157, for 'He is a very proper man', you could say 'He is very good-looking'.

c. Read aloud lines 154–161 again. This time, the person playing Benedick should echo out loud the word or phrase that affects Benedick most from each thing that he hears.

d. Discuss and agree why the other characters say these things about Benedick in this situation. What are they trying to do to him with the words? This is the tactic behind the words. For example, for 'proper' in line 157, Claudio's tactic might be to flatter him.

e. Read lines 154–161 again. This time, each character should try to make their tactics **explicit** in the way they speak their lines.

f. Write a paragraph explaining what the language each character uses reveals about their tactics.

Glossary

146 **dotage** devotion
147 **doffed** put aside
152 **bate** stop
154 **make tender of** offer
157 **proper** good-looking
162 **Hector** brave Trojan champion (in mythology)
168 **large** improper
171 **wear it out** get over it

Key term

Explicit clear and open

Don Pedro   I would she had bestowed this dotage on me. I would have
doffed all other respects and made her half myself. I pray you,
tell Benedick of it and hear what he will say.

Leonato   Were it good, think you?

Claudio   Hero thinks surely she will die, for she says she will die if he love   150
her not, and she will die ere she make her love known, and she
will die, if he woo her, rather than she will bate one breath of
her accustomed crossness.

Don Pedro   She doth well. If she should make tender of her love 'tis very
possible he'll scorn it, for the man, as you know all, hath a   155
contemptible spirit.

Claudio   He is a very proper man.

Don Pedro   He hath indeed a good outward happiness.

Claudio   Before God, and, in my mind, very wise.

Don Pedro   He doth indeed show some sparks that are like wit.   160

Claudio   And I take him to be valiant.

Don Pedro   As Hector, I assure you. And in the managing of quarrels
you may say he is wise, for either he avoids them with great
discretion, or undertakes them with a most Christianlike fear.

Leonato   If he do fear God, a must necessarily keep peace. If he break the   165
peace, he ought to enter into a quarrel with fear and trembling.

Don Pedro   And so will he do, for the man doth fear God, howsoever it
seems not in him by some large jests he will make. Well, I am
sorry for your niece. Shall we go seek Benedick and tell him of
her love?   170

Claudio   Never tell him, my lord. Let her wear it out with good counsel.

Leonato   Nay, that's impossible. She may wear her heart out first.

Don Pedro   Well, we will hear further of it by your daughter. Let it cool the
while. I love Benedick well and I could wish he would modestly
examine himself to see how much he is unworthy so good a   175
lady.

Don Pedro, Claudio and Leonato leave Benedick alone. He shares with the audience his thoughts and feelings about Beatrice, and decides that he loves her. Beatrice comes in and tells him it is dinner time.

Did you know?

Actors often physically explore the punctuation in a speech to help them connect with the way their character is thinking and feeling.

Glossary

182–183 **no such matter** there will be nothing in it
184 **a dumb show** speechless
185 **sadly** seriously
187 **full bent** fully stretched (like an archer's bow)
196 **horribly** totally
201–202 **career of his humour** pursuit of his mood

Activity 7: Exploring punctuation

a. Read lines 185–205. As you read aloud, stand up on the first full stop, sit down on the next one and then continue standing up or sitting down every time you come to a full stop. Treat the question marks in the same way. When you come to a comma, stamp your foot.

b. Join up with a partner and discuss what impact the use of punctuation has in this speech. The punctuation is an indicator of a character moving from one thought to another. What state of mind would you say Benedick is in? How do you think he is feeling during this speech? Why might that be?

c. Write a paragraph or two explaining what you think Benedick's state of mind is at this stage in the play. Use evidence from lines 185–205 in your writing.

Benedick, 2014

Leonato   My lord, will you walk? Dinner is ready.

Claudio   [Aside] If he do not dote on her upon this, I will never trust my
expectation.

Don Pedro   [Aside] Let there be the same net spread for her, and that must   180
your daughter and her gentlewomen carry. The sport will be
when they hold one an opinion of another's dotage, and no such
matter. That's the scene that I would see, which will be merely
a dumb show. Let us send her to call him in to dinner.

Exeunt Don Pedro, Claudio and Leonato

Benedick   This can be no trick. The conference was sadly borne. They   185
have the truth of this from Hero. They seem to pity the lady. It
seems her affections have their full bent. Love me? Why, it must
be requited. I hear how I am censured. They say I will bear
myself proudly if I perceive the love come from her. They say
too that she will rather die than give any sign of affection. I did   190
never think to marry. I must not seem proud. Happy are they
that hear their detractions and can put them to mending. They
say the lady is fair. 'Tis a truth, I can bear them witness. And
virtuous. 'Tis so, I cannot reprove it. And wise, but for loving me.
By my troth, it is no addition to her wit, nor no great argument   195
of her folly, for I will be horribly in love with her. I may chance
have some odd quirks and remnants of wit broken on me
because I have railed so long against marriage, but doth not
the appetite alter? A man loves the meat in his youth that he
cannot endure in his age. Shall quips and sentences and these   200
paper bullets of the brain awe a man from the career of his
humour? No. The world must be peopled. When I said I would
die a bachelor, I did not think I should live till I were married.
Here comes Beatrice. By this day, she's a fair lady. I do spy some
marks of love in her.   205

Enter Beatrice

Beatrice   Against my will I am sent to bid you come in to dinner.

Benedick   Fair Beatrice, I thank you for your pains.

Beatrice leaves and Benedick considers every word she has just said to him, as he searches for indicators that she loves him. He goes off to get a picture of Beatrice, his love.

Glossary

212 **daw** jackdaw

212 **no stomach** no appetite

218–219 **I am a Jew** An insulting comment in Shakespeare's time, meaning I am not to be believed

219 **picture** a miniature portrait, which he would probably wear

Activity 8: Exploring Benedick

Look at the photo on this page of Benedick in the 2014 RSC production and discuss the following questions.

   i. What do you think Benedick is feeling at the end of Act 2 Scene 3?

   ii. What has made him feel this way?

   iii. Why do you think Benedick decides to go and get a miniature picture of Beatrice?

   iv. What is your opinion of Benedick at the end of Act 2 Scene 3?

Beatrice I took no more pains for those thanks than you take pains to thank me. If it had been painful I would not have come.

Benedick You take pleasure, then, in the message?   210

Beatrice Yea, just so much as you may take upon a knife's point and choke a daw withal. You have no stomach, signor? Fare you well.

Exit Beatrice

Benedick Ha! 'Against my will I am sent to bid you come in to dinner.' There's a double meaning in that. 'I took no more pains for   215 those thanks than you took pains to thank me.' That's as much as to say 'Any pains that I take for you is as easy as thanks.' If I do not take pity of her I am a villain. If I do not love her, I am a Jew. I will go get her picture.

Exit Benedick

Exploring Act 2

Beatrice and Benedick, 2006

Activity 1: Designing Act 2

Look back over Act 2. Use the page summaries to help you remember what happens.

a. Where does the action of Act 2 take place? Imagine you are the designer of a production of *Much Ado About Nothing*. Write down all the locations for the action that you would need. For example, you might include the place in which the masked dancing in Act 2 Scene 1 happens. Remember, you also need to include something that Benedick can hide behind.

b. What are the essential **props** for Act 2? Write a list of props you would need. For example, you might include the masks that are worn by the characters in Act 2 Scene 1.

c. What would you say was the overall mood of Act 2? What colours might suit that mood?

d. Write notes on, draw or make a model of your stage design for Act 2.

Key term

Prop an object used in the play, e.g. a dagger

Did you know?

Theatre designers start by investigating the script of the play. They work with the director to build a three-dimensional world in which the action of the play can take place. Their choice of colours, locations and props helps the audience to understand the action of the play.

Activity 2: Exploring the theme of deception

a. Discuss how Shakespeare develops the theme of deception in Act 2. Copy and complete the diagram below, which divides the characters in Act 2 into 'Deceivers' and 'Deceived'. You could add arrows to your diagram to show who is deceiving whom and why you think they are doing that.

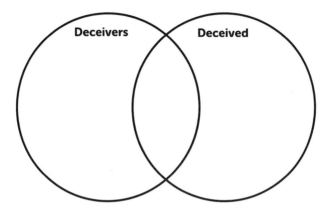

b. Discuss your choices. Are there any characters you have placed in both categories (where the circles overlap)?

c. Discuss how you think the deceptions that have been set up will develop in Act 3.

Leonato, Claudio and Don Pedro, 2006

In the orchard, Hero, Margaret and Ursula plan how they will get Beatrice to admit that she is in love with Benedick. Hero sends Margaret to fetch Beatrice and then instructs Ursula in what their conversation should be.

Margaret and Hero, 2006

Glossary

3 **Proposing** talking

7 **pleachèd bower** place with closely woven hedges

16 **trace** pace

24 **lapwing** a type of bird that runs along the ground to draw predators away from its nest

25 **conference** conversation

Did you know?

Actors in rehearsal sometimes improvise a scene as if it is happening now, using their own words, but keeping the same characters and situation from Shakespeare's original play. They do this to help them connect directly with the **themes** and ideas in the scene.

Activity 1: Exploring Hero's plan

a. In small groups, read aloud lines 1–13, swapping readers at the punctuation marks.

b. Choose one person who will read aloud lines 1–13 as if they are Hero. The rest of the group should act out Hero's plan silently, playing all the characters that Hero mentions.

c. Divide into pairs and read aloud lines 15–23, swapping readers at the punctuation marks.

d. In your pairs, **improvise** the conversation that Hero proposes in lines 15–23 as if you are Hero and Ursula, and Beatrice is listening. Ursula should praise Benedick, while Hero should talk about how much in love with Beatrice he is.

e. Write a paragraph that explains Hero's plan in detail, using evidence from lines 1–23 in your explanation.

Key terms

Improvise make up in the moment

Theme the main ideas explored in a piece of literature, e.g. the themes of love and marriage, male and female relationships, deception, loyalty and honour might be considered key themes of *Much Ado About Nothing*

Act 3 | Scene 1

Enter Hero, Margaret and Ursula

Hero   Good Margaret, run thee to the parlour.
There shalt thou find my cousin Beatrice
Proposing with the Prince and Claudio.
Whisper her ear, and tell her I and Ursula
Walk in the orchard, and our whole discourse   5
Is all of her. Say that thou overheard'st us.
And bid her steal into the pleachèd bower
Where honeysuckles, ripened by the sun,
Forbid the sun to enter, like favourites
Made proud by princes, that advance their pride   10
Against that power that bred it. There will she hide her
To listen our purpose. This is thy office.
Bear thee well in it, and leave us alone.

Margaret   I'll make her come, I warrant you, presently.

Exit Margaret

Hero   Now, Ursula, when Beatrice doth come,   15
As we do trace this alley up and down
Our talk must only be of Benedick.
When I do name him, let it be thy part
To praise him more than ever man did merit.
My talk to thee must be how Benedick   20
Is sick in love with Beatrice. Of this matter
Is little Cupid's crafty arrow made,
That only wounds by hearsay.

Enter Beatrice

                  Now begin.
For look where Beatrice, like a lapwing, runs
Close by the ground to hear our conference.   25

Ursula   The pleasant'st angling is to see the fish
Cut with her golden oars the silver stream

Ursula reassures Hero that she will play her part in the trick. They move closer to where Beatrice is hiding, speaking of Benedick's supposed love for Beatrice. Hero suggests that Beatrice loves herself so much that she is incapable of loving someone else.

Activity 2: Exploring the theme of deception

a. In groups, decide who will play Ursula, Hero and Beatrice. Read aloud lines 26–33. Beatrice does not speak but should listen to the other characters.

b. In lines 26–33, Ursula and Hero use an **extended metaphor** for the trick they are about to play on Beatrice. Pick out all the words that are related to fishing.

c. Read lines 34–56, but this time the people playing Ursula and Hero should hit their script with their hand every time they think they have said something that would make Beatrice take the 'bait' they are laying for her. For example, the person playing Hero might hit the script when Hero says 'she is too disdainful' in line 34.

d. Discuss and decide what Beatrice is thinking and feeling during lines 34–56. What does her expression in the photo on this page suggest about her feelings? Think about how the theme of deception is presented in these lines.

e. Write a diary entry for Beatrice in modern English as if she has just overheard the conversation between Hero and Ursula in lines 34–56. Include the words that had the most powerful effect on her.

Glossary

30 **couchèd** lying
30 **woodbine coverture** honeysuckle shelter
35 **coy** contrary
36 **haggards** wild hawks
38 **new trothèd** recently engaged
52 **Misprising** undervaluing
54 **All matter** everything
55 **shape** image
55 **project** idea
56 **self-endeared** in love with herself

Key term

Extended metaphor describing something by comparing it to something else over several lines

And greedily devour the treacherous bait.
So angle we for Beatrice, who even now
Is couchèd in the woodbine coverture.   30
Fear you not my part of the dialogue.

Hero   Then go we near her, that her ear lose nothing
Of the false-sweet bait that we lay for it.
No, truly, Ursula, she is too disdainful.
I know her spirits are as coy and wild   35
As haggards of the rock.

Ursula   But are you sure
That Benedick loves Beatrice so entirely?

Hero   So says the Prince and my new trothèd lord.

Ursula   And did they bid you tell her of it, madam?

Hero   They did entreat me to acquaint her of it,   40
But I persuaded them, if they loved Benedick,
To wish him wrestle with affection
And never to let Beatrice know of it.

Ursula   Why did you so? Doth not the gentleman
Deserve as full as fortunate a bed   45
As ever Beatrice shall couch upon?

Hero   O god of love! I know he doth deserve
As much as may be yielded to a man.
But nature never framed a woman's heart
Of prouder stuff than that of Beatrice.   50
Disdain and scorn ride sparkling in her eyes,
Misprising what they look on, and her wit
Values itself so highly that to her
All matter else seems weak. She cannot love,
Nor take no shape nor project of affection,   55
She is so self-endeared.

Ursula   Sure, I think so.
And therefore certainly it were not good
She knew his love, lest she make sport at it.

Knowing that Beatrice can hear every word they are saying, Hero and Ursula continue. Hero outlines all the ways in which Beatrice has undermined men and mocked those who challenge her. Ursula suggests that Hero tell Beatrice that Benedick is in love with her, but Hero says she will tell Benedick that her cousin is not worthy of him to save him from getting hurt by Beatrice.

Beatrice, Ursula and Hero, 2006

Key terms

Statue like a freeze-frame but usually of a single character

Antithesis bringing two opposing concepts or ideas together, e.g. hot and cold, love and hate, loud and quiet

Activity 3: Exploring antithesis

a. In pairs, read aloud lines 59–70, swapping readers at the end of each sentence.

b. Using the glossary box, put lines 59–70 into your own words.

c. List all the types of men that are mentioned in lines 59–70.

d. Using **statues**, one of you should show each type of man mentioned and the other show how Beatrice would twist his good quality and make it negative. For example, for line 65, one of you could show a short, confident man and the other show a short, misshapen man.

e. Write one or two paragraphs that explain how Shakespeare's use of **antithesis** in lines 59–70 helps to make what Hero is saying funny.

Glossary

61 **spell him backward** take him the wrong way

63 **black** dark

64 **lance ill-headed** spear with an ineffective head

65 **agate** a semi-precious gemstone

66 **vane** weathervane

70 **purchaseth** earns

76 **press… wit** Pressing to death was a punishment for criminals who refused to speak in court

84 **honest slanders** harmless lies

Did you know?

Actors sometimes explore antithesis in rehearsals by physically acting out the opposing concepts that are contained in their lines. They do this so that they can feel the tension between the opposites as they speak.

Hero Why, you speak truth. I never yet saw man,
How wise, how noble, young, how rarely featured,   60
But she would spell him backward. If fair-faced,
She would swear the gentleman should be her sister;
If black, why, nature, drawing of an antic,
Made a foul blot. If tall, a lance ill-headed;
If low, an agate very vilely cut.   65
If speaking, why, a vane blown with all winds;
If silent, why, a block movèd with none.
So turns she every man the wrong side out,
And never gives to truth and virtue that
Which simpleness and merit purchaseth.   70

Ursula Sure, sure, such carping is not commendable.

Hero No, not to be so odd and from all fashions
As Beatrice is cannot be commendable.
But who dare tell her so? If I should speak
She would mock me into air. O she would laugh me   75
Out of myself, press me to death with wit.
Therefore let Benedick, like covered fire,
Consume away in sighs, waste inwardly.
It were a better death than die with mocks,
Which is as bad as die with tickling.   80

Ursula Yet tell her of it. Hear what she will say.

Hero No, rather I will go to Benedick
And counsel him to fight against his passion.
And truly, I'll devise some honest slanders
To stain my cousin with. One doth not know   85
How much an ill word may empoison liking.

Ursula O do not do your cousin such a wrong.
She cannot be so much without true judgement,
Having so swift and excellent a wit
As she is prized to have, as to refuse   90
So rare a gentleman as Signor Benedick.

and Ursula praise Benedick before going in to look at Hero's wedding clothes.
en they have gone, Beatrice shares her thoughts and feelings with the audience,
coming Benedick's love and saying she wants to marry him.

Beatrice, 2012

Activity 4: Exploring rhythm and rhyme

a. Stand up and read aloud lines 107–116 while stamping the rhythm of the words with your feet, emphasising the strong beats as if you are a galloping horse.

b. Most of what Beatrice says in lines 107–116 fits the **iambic pentameter** rhythm quite naturally, but the word 'Taming' in line 112 does not.

i. Read the word 'taming' out loud. Which part of the word do you naturally emphasise?

ii. When there is a variation in the rhythm like this, it makes the word on which it happens stand out. Why might Shakespeare have wanted the word 'taming' to stand out?

Key terms

Iambic pentameter the rhythm Shakespeare uses to write his plays. Each line in this rhythm contains approximately ten **syllables**. 'Iambic' means putting the stress on the second syllable of each beat. 'Pentameter' means five beats with two syllables in each beat

Syllable part of a word that is one sound, e.g. 'highness' has two syllables – 'high' and 'ness'

Hero He is the only man of Italy,
Always excepted my dear Claudio.

Ursula I pray you be not angry with me, madam,
Speaking my fancy. Signor Benedick,   95
For shape, for bearing, argument, and valour,
Goes foremost in report through Italy.

Hero Indeed, he hath an excellent good name.

Ursula His excellence did earn it ere he had it.
When are you married, madam?   100

Hero Why, every day, tomorrow. Come, go in.
I'll show thee some attires and have thy counsel
Which is the best to furnish me tomorrow.

Ursula (Aside) She's limed, I warrant you. We have caught her, madam.

Hero (Aside) If it proves so, then loving goes by haps.   105
Some Cupid kills with arrows, some with traps.

Exeunt Hero and Ursula

Beatrice What fire is in mine ears? Can this be true?
Stand I condemned for pride and scorn so much?
Contempt, farewell, and maiden pride, adieu.
No glory lives behind the back of such.   110
And, Benedick, love on, I will requite thee,
Taming my wild heart to thy loving hand.
If thou dost love, my kindness shall incite thee
To bind our loves up in a holy band.
For others say thou dost deserve, and I   115
Believe it better than reportingly.

Exit Beatrice

Don Pedro, Claudio and Leonato notice that Benedick is behaving differently. Benedick says he has toothache, but Claudio suggests Benedick is in love.

Claudio, Benedick and Don Pedro, 2006

Activity 1: Exploring the theme of love

a. In small groups, decide who will play Don Pedro, Claudio, Leonato and Benedick. Read aloud lines 12–24.

b. Stand in a square, a few steps apart. To help you understand more about the characters, their relationships and their motives, read lines 12–24 again. This time, as you speak and listen, you should keep choosing between the following movements:
   • Take a step towards another character.
   • Take a step away from another character.
   • Turn towards another character.
   • Turn away from another character.
   • Stand still.
   Try to make instinctive choices rather than planning what to do.

c. Look at the photo on this page. Which line do you think is being spoken here? Explain your reasons.

d. How would you describe the relationship between the characters in lines 12–24?

e. Write a commentary describing what you think is happening between Benedick and the other three characters in lines 12–24 and explaining each character's attitude to love at this point in the play.

Glossary

3 **vouchsafe** permit

8–9 **little hangman** Cupid

15 **truant** rogue

15–18 **Hang… Draw it** Hanging and drawing (disembowelling) were punishments for criminals

22 **worm** The Elizabethans believed that toothache was caused by worms breeding in the rotten moisture of a hollow tooth

At the time

Using page 203, find out what the Elizabethans believed were the signs of love.

Act 3 | Scene 2

Enter Don Pedro, Claudio, Benedick and Leonato

Don Pedro I do but stay till your marriage be consummate, and then go
I toward Aragon.

Claudio I'll bring you thither, my lord, if you'll vouchsafe me.

Don Pedro Nay, that would be as great a soil in the new gloss of your
marriage as to show a child his new coat and forbid him to   5
wear it. I will only be bold with Benedick for his company, for
from the crown of his head to the sole of his foot, he is all mirth.
He hath twice or thrice cut Cupid's bow-string and the little
hangman dare not shoot at him. He hath a heart as sound as a
bell, and his tongue is the clapper, for what his heart thinks his   10
tongue speaks.

Benedick Gallants, I am not as I have been.

Leonato So say I, methinks you are sadder.

Claudio I hope he be in love.

Don Pedro Hang him, truant. There's no true drop of blood in him to be   15
truly touched with love. If he be sad, he wants money.

Benedick I have the toothache.

Don Pedro Draw it.

Benedick Hang it.

Claudio You must hang it first and draw it afterwards.   20

Don Pedro What? Sigh for the toothache?

Leonato Where is but a humour or a worm.

Benedick Well, everyone can master a grief but he that has it.

Claudio Yet say I he is in love.

Claudio, Leonato and Don Pedro comment on the detail of Benedick's changed appearance. Benedick escapes by asking for a private chat with Leonato. Don Pedro and Claudio congratulate themselves on convincing Benedick that Beatrice is in love with him.

Don Pedro, Benedick and Leonato, 2014

Activity 2: Exploring the character of Benedick

a. In groups, decide who will play Claudio, Don Pedro, Leonato and Benedick (who remains silent). Read aloud lines 30–44.

b. Look at the photo on this page from the 2014 RSC production. Which line from lines 30–44 do you think is being spoken in this photo? Explain your reasons. How do you think Benedick feels at this moment? Why do you think he feels that way?

c. Select a line each from lines 30–44 for the people playing Claudio, Don Pedro and Leonato. Choose the lines you think will have the strongest effect on Benedick.

d. Decide on a **gesture** that each character might make towards Benedick while they say their chosen line.

e. The person playing Benedick should stand in the middle with the people playing the other characters standing around them. Each character should speak their line from task c to Benedick while Benedick reacts.

f. Go back through lines 30–44 and decide what Benedick is thinking at each moment. Write down those thoughts in your own words.

Glossary

25 **fancy** affection
26 **strange disguises** foreign fashions
31 **A** he
34 **ornament of his cheek** beard
34 **stuffed tennis balls** Tennis balls were made of leather stuffed with hair
36 **civet** musky perfume from a civet cat
42 **crept into a lute-string** singing love songs
43 **stops** frets on a lute
48 **buried with her face upwards** smothered
51 **hobby-horses** ridiculous toy horses worn around the waist of Morris dancers

Key term

Gesture a movement, often using the hands or head, to express a feeling or idea

Don Pedro There is no appearance of fancy in him, unless it be a fancy   25
that he hath to strange disguises, as to be a Dutchman today, a
Frenchman tomorrow. Unless he have a fancy to this foolery, as
it appears he hath, he is no fool for fancy, as you would have it
appear he is.

Claudio If he be not in love with some woman, there is no believing old   30
signs. A brushes his hat o' mornings. What should that bode?

Don Pedro Hath any man seen him at the barber's?

Claudio No, but the barber's man hath been seen with him and the old
ornament of his cheek hath already stuffed tennis balls.

Leonato Indeed, he looks younger than he did, by the loss of a beard.   35

Don Pedro Nay, a rubs himself with civet. Can you smell him out by that?

Claudio That's as much as to say, the sweet youth's in love.

Don Pedro The greatest note of it is his melancholy.

Claudio And when was he wont to wash his face?

Don Pedro Yea, or to paint himself? For the which I hear what they say   40
of him.

Claudio Nay, but his jesting spirit, which is now crept into a lute-string,
and now governed by stops.

Don Pedro Indeed, that tells a heavy tale for him. Conclude, he is in love.

Claudio Nay, but I know who loves him.   45

Don Pedro That would I know, too. I warrant, one that knows him not.

Claudio Yes, and his ill conditions, and in despite of all, dies for him.

Don Pedro She shall be buried with her face upwards.

Benedick Yet is this no charm for the toothache. Old signor, walk aside
with me. I have studied eight or nine wise words to speak to   50
you, which these hobby-horses must not hear.

Exeunt Benedick and Leonato

It is the night before Claudio's wedding to Hero. Don John comes in, tells Don Pedro and Claudio that Hero is unfaithful, and asks them to go with him later that night to see a strange man enter her bedroom window.

Activity 3: Exploring the theme of deception

a. In small groups, decide who will play Don John, Don Pedro and Claudio. Read aloud lines 72–92.

b. Give the person playing Don John a handful of playing cards or slips of paper. Read lines 72–84 again. This time, the person playing Don John should give a card or paper to one of the other characters every time he says something that has an effect on them. Think about the manner in which Don John gives the card. For example, in line 74, when Don John says 'the lady is disloyal', he might play that card on Claudio, directly in his face, or he might play it on Don Pedro by slipping it discreetly to him.

c. Read lines 72–84 again, with the person playing Don John giving out the cards in the same way. This time, the people playing Don Pedro and Claudio should decide whether or not to take the cards that they are offered and the manner in which to take them.

d. Write a paragraph that explains the **tactics** that Don John uses to deceive Claudio and Don Pedro during lines 72–92.

Don John, 2006

Glossary

68 **aim better at me** judge me better
68 **manifest** show
69 **holds you well** thinks well of you
69 **holp** helped
73 **circumstances shortened** cutting a long story short

Key term

Tactics the method a character uses to get what they want

Don Pedro	For my life, to break with him about Beatrice.
Claudio	'Tis even so. Hero and Margaret have by this played their parts with Beatrice, and then the two bears will not bite one another when they meet. 55

Enter Don John

Don John	My lord, and brother, God save you.
Don Pedro	Good den, brother.
Don John	If your leisure served, I would speak with you.
Don Pedro	In private?
Don John	If it please you. Yet Count Claudio may hear, for what I would 60 speak of concerns him.
Don Pedro	What's the matter?
Don John	Means your lordship to be married tomorrow?
Don Pedro	You know he does.
Don John	I know not that when he knows what I know. 65
Claudio	If there be any impediment, I pray you discover it.
Don John	You may think I love you not. Let that appear hereafter, and aim better at me by that I now will manifest. For my brother – I think he holds you well and in dearness of heart – hath holp to effect your ensuing marriage – surely suit ill spent and labour ill 70 bestowed.
Don Pedro	Why, what's the matter?
Don John	I came hither to tell you, and, circumstances shortened – for she has been too long a-talking of – the lady is disloyal.
Claudio	Who, Hero? 75
Don Pedro	Even she. Leonato's Hero, your Hero, every man's Hero.
Claudio	Disloyal?

...dio and Don Pedro agree to go with Don John at midnight to Hero's chamber window
...ee if what he is saying is true. Claudio declares that if he sees Hero being unfaithful, he
...shame her on their wedding day in front of the whole congregation.

Don John, 2006

t the time

Using page 207, find out
about the importance of
the code of honour. In
what ways might the code
of honour guide people's
behaviour? Was the idea of
honour different for men and
women?

Activity 4: Exploring the theme of honour

a. Look back at the whole of Act 3 Scene 2. In what ways
   are Benedick and Claudio changed during this scene?
b. In line 83, Don John says honour is the reason why
   Claudio should not marry Hero. The word 'honour' is
   still used today. What do you think makes someone
   honourable nowadays? Is honour different for men
   and women?
c. Would you say Benedick or Claudio was the most
   honourable man in Act 3 Scene 2? Give reasons for
   your suggestion.
d. Imagining you are Claudio, write a letter in modern
   English to Don Pedro, using the idea of honour to
   explain the reasons for your actions in Act 3 Scene 2.

Don John   The word is too good to paint out her wickedness. I could say
she were worse. Think you of a worse title, and I will fit her to
it. Wonder not till further warrant. Go but with me tonight, you   80
shall see her chamber window entered, even the night before
her wedding day. If you love her then, tomorrow wed her. But it
would better fit your honour to change your mind.

Claudio   May this be so?

Don Pedro   I will not think it.   85

Don John   If you dare not trust that you see, confess not that you know.
If you will follow me, I will show you enough, and when you
have seen more and heard more, proceed accordingly.

Claudio   If I see any thing tonight why I should not marry her, tomorrow,
in the congregation, where I should wed, there will I shame her.   90

Don Pedro   And, as I wooed for thee to obtain her, I will join with thee to
disgrace her.

Don John   I will disparage her no farther till you are my witnesses. Bear it
coldly but till midnight, and let the issue show itself.

Don Pedro   O day untowardly turned!   95

Claudio   O mischief strangely thwarting!

Don John   O plague right well prevented! So will you say when you have
seen the sequel.

Exeunt

Dogberry and Verges meet with the men of the Watch to choose a Constable, and brief the Watch on how they should behave as officers of the law.

Second Watchman and Dogberry, 2014

At the time

Using page 201, find out about the Watch in Elizabethan England. How was the Watch different from the police force today?

Activity 1: Exploring a comic scene

a. In groups, decide who will play Dogberry, Verges and the First Watchman. Read aloud lines 1–13. This is the first time in the play that we meet these characters.

b. In line 2, Verges says 'salvation' when he actually means 'damnation'. How does this **malapropism** help to make the opening of Act 3 Scene 3 funny?

c. Go through lines 1–13 and find two other examples of Verges or Dogberry saying one thing and meaning something completely different that sounds similar.

d. Look at the photo on this page. Why do you think the Watchman is carrying a rake? How does Dogberry's physical position make him funny?

e. Imagine that Dogberry has put a notice up to recruit volunteers for the Watch. Make that notice, using malapropisms in your work.

Glossary

2 **salvation** This is a malapropism for 'damnation'
7 **charge** duties
8 **constable** an official who is responsible for public order
12 **well-favoured** good-looking
20 **vagrom** homeless and unemployed (vagrant)
22 **a** he

Key term

Malapropism mistaken use of a word that sounds like another word but has a very different meaning

Act 3 | Scene 3

Enter Dogberry, Verges and the Watch

Dogberry Are you good men and true?

Verges Yea, or else it were pity but they should suffer salvation, body and soul.

Dogberry Nay, that were a punishment too good for them if they should have any allegiance in them, being chosen for the Prince's watch. 5

Verges Well, give them their charge, neighbour Dogberry.

Dogberry First, who think you the most desertless man to be constable?

First Watchman Hugh Oatcake, sir, or George Seacole, for they can write and read. 10

Dogberry Come hither, neighbour Seacole. God hath blest you with a good name. To be a well-favoured man is the gift of fortune, but to write and read comes by nature.

Second Watchman Both which, Master Constable—

Dogberry You have. I knew it would be your answer. Well, for your favour, 15 sir, why, give God thanks, and make no boast of it. And for your writing and reading, let that appear when there is no need of such vanity. You are thought here to be the most senseless and fit man for the constable of the watch, therefore bear you the lantern. This is your charge: you shall comprehend all vagrom 20 men. You are to bid any man stand, in the Prince's name.

Second Watchman How if a will not stand?

Dogberry Why then take no note of him, but let him go, and presently call the rest of the watch together, and thank God you are rid of a knave. 25

Verges If he will not stand when he is bidden he is none of the Prince's subjects.

Dogberry and Verges continue to instruct the Watch on how they should deal with drunks, thieves and disturbances of the peace.

Activity 2: Exploring physical comedy

a. In pairs, read aloud lines 35–38 with one of you as Dogberry and the other as the Second Watchman. Start where Dogberry says 'Well, you are to call at all the alehouses' and finish when Dogberry says 'till they are sober'.

b. Join another pair and create a **freeze-frame**, in which one of you is the Second Watchman, two of you are drunkards and one of you is Dogberry watching from a distance.

c. Bring your freeze-frame to life by speaking lines 35–38. As you speak, show the Second Watchman calling at the alehouse, bidding the drunkards to get to bed, the drunkards refusing and the Second Watchman then leaving them alone until they are sober. Make sure that the attitudes of all the characters are clear. Freeze again when you have finished speaking the lines.

d. Now decide who will play Dogberry, Verges and the Second Watchman. Read aloud lines 45–58.

e. Discuss the advice Dogberry gives for dealing with other petty crimes in this section of the scene.

f. Imagine the Watchmen have to write a report at the end of their shift. Write your report in modern English as if you are a Watchman who has followed one of Dogberry's pieces of advice.

Dogberry, 2006

Glossary

33 **ancient** experienced
35 **bills** long-handled, axe-headed tools
46 **pitch** tar

Key term

Freeze-frame a physical, still image created by people to represent an object, place, person or feeling

Dogberry True, and they are to meddle with none but the Prince's subjects.
You shall also make no noise in the streets, for, for the watch to
babble and to talk is most tolerable and not to be endured. 30

First Watchman We will rather sleep than talk. We know what belongs to a
watch.

Dogberry Why, you speak like an ancient and most quiet watchman, for
I cannot see how sleeping should offend. Only have a care that
your bills be not stolen. Well, you are to call at all the alehouses 35
and bid those that are drunk get them to bed.

Second Watchman How if they will not?

Dogberry Why then, let them alone till they are sober. If they make you
not then the better answer, you may say they are not the men
you took them for. 40

Second Watchman Well, sir.

Dogberry If you meet a thief, you may suspect him, by virtue of your
office, to be no true man, and, for such kind of men, the less you
meddle or make with them why, the more is for your honesty.

Second Watchman If we know him to be a thief, shall we not lay hands on him? 45

Dogberry Truly, by your office you may, but I think they that touch pitch
will be defiled. The most peaceable way for you if you do take a
thief is to let him show himself what he is, and steal out of your
company.

Verges You have been always called a merciful man, partner. 50

Dogberry Truly, I would not hang a dog by my will, much more a man
who hath any honesty in him.

Verges If you hear a child cry in the night, you must call to the nurse
and bid her still it.

Second Watchman How if the nurse be asleep and will not hear us? 55

Dogberry Why then, depart in peace and let the child wake her with
crying, for the ewe that will not hear her lamb when it baas will
never answer a calf when he bleats.

Before going to bed, Dogberry and Verges instruct the Watch to keep a close watch on Leonato's house because it is the night before the wedding. The Watchmen hide when Conrad and Borachio come in. Borachio tells Conrad that he has earned a thousand gold coins from Don John for the villainy he has done this night.

The Watchmen, 2006

Activity 3: Exploring the structure of a scene

a. In pairs, read aloud lines 77–91 with one of you as Conrad and the other as Borachio, missing out the Second Watchman's lines 78 and 86.

b. Read lines 77–91 again, this time as if you are keeping a secret and do not want to be overheard.

c. In line 85, Borachio says he will tell Conrad everything he has been up to 'like a true drunkard'. Read lines 77–91 again, this time as if Borachio is drunk and loud, but Conrad is trying to keep him quiet.

d. Join up with another pair and decide who will play the hiding Watchmen. Read lines 77–91 again, this time including the Watchmen's lines as if they are hiding and do not want Conrad and Borachio to hear them.

e. Prepare your version of lines 77–91 and then share this with the rest of the class.

Glossary

60 **present** represent

76 **coil** commotion

76 **vigitant** This is a malapropism for 'vigilant'

81 **Mass** by the mass (mild swearing)

81 **my elbow itched** Proverbially, this was a warning of evil or danger

81 **scab** scoundrel, and the result of scratching the itch

84 **penthouse** overhang

Verges   'Tis very true.

Dogberry   This is the end of the charge. You, constable, are to present the   60
Prince's own person. If you meet the Prince in the night you
may stay him.

Verges   Nay, by'r Lady, that I think a cannot.

Dogberry   Five shillings to one on't, with any man that knows the statues,
he may stay him. Marry, not without the Prince be willing, for   65
indeed the watch ought to offend no man, and it is an offence
to stay a man against his will.

Verges   By'r Lady, I think it be so.

Dogberry   Ha, ah ha! Well, masters, good night. And there be any matter
of weight chances, call up me. Keep your fellows' counsels, and   70
your own, and good night. Come, neighbour.

First Watchman   Well, masters, we hear our charge. Let us go sit here upon the
church bench till two, and then all to bed.

Dogberry   One word more, honest neighbours. I pray you watch about
Signor Leonato's door, for the wedding being there tomorrow,   75
there is a great coil tonight. Adieu. Be vigitant, I beseech you.

Exeunt Dogberry and Verges. Enter Borachio and Conrad

Borachio   What, Conrad?

Second Watchman   [Aside] Peace, stir not.

Borachio   Conrad, I say!

Conrad   Here, man, I am at thy elbow.   80

Borachio   Mass, and my elbow itched, I thought there would a scab follow.

Conrad   I will owe thee an answer for that. And now, forward with
thy tale.

Borachio   Stand thee close, then, under this penthouse, for it drizzles rain,
and I will, like a true drunkard, utter all to thee.   85

Second Watchman   [Aside] Some treason, masters. Yet stand close.

While the Watchmen watch, Borachio talks about fashion until Conrad reminds him to tell the story of what he was doing earlier. Borachio reveals that he has deliberately misled Don Pedro and Claudio by wooing Margaret (trying to make her fall in love with him), who was pretending to be Hero, at Hero's bedroom window.

Borachio and Conrad, 2014

Activity 4: Exploring the Royal Shakespeare Theatre stage

a. Look at the photo on this page of Conrad and Borachio in Act 3 Scene 3. Is this how you imagine the scene? Give reasons for your answer.

b. Look closely at the Royal Shakespeare Theatre stage behind the actors. Decide where you think the Watchmen should be hiding. Write a paragraph describing how you would stage lines 77–115, explaining your choices.

Glossary

91 **make** ask

93 **unconfirmed** inexperienced

94 **is nothing to a man** tells you nothing about a man

99 **deformed** absurd

107–108 **Pharaoh's soldiers** the soldiers who drowned in the Red Sea chasing Moses (from the Bible)

108 **reechy** dirty

108 **god Bel's priests** priests who were killed by the king of Persia for worshipping a false god (from the Bible)

110 **codpiece** decorative pouch worn on the front of a man's trousers

Borachio   Therefore, know I have earned of Don John a thousand ducats.

Conrad   Is it possible that any villainy should be so dear?

Borachio   Thou shouldst rather ask if it were possible any villainy should
be so rich. For when rich villains have need of poor ones, poor   90
ones may make what price they will.

Conrad   I wonder at it.

Borachio   That shows thou art unconfirmed. Thou know'st that the fashion
of a doublet, or a hat, or a cloak is nothing to a man.

Conrad   Yes, it is apparel.   95

Borachio   I mean the fashion.

Conrad   Yes, the fashion is the fashion.

Borachio   Tush, I may as well say the fool's the fool. But seest thou not
what a deformed thief this fashion is?

First Watchman   [Aside] I know that Deformed. A has been a vile thief this   100
seven year. A goes up and down like a gentleman. I remember
his name.

Borachio   Didst thou not hear somebody?

Conrad   No, 'twas the vane on the house.

Borachio   Seest thou not, I say, what a deformed thief this fashion is,   105
how giddily a turns about all the hot-bloods between fourteen
and five-and-thirty, sometimes fashioning them like Pharaoh's
soldiers in the reechy painting, sometime like god Bel's priests
in the old church-window, sometime like the shaven Hercules in
the smirched, worm-eaten tapestry, where his codpiece seems as   110
massy as his club.

Conrad   All this I see, and I see that the fashion wears out more apparel
than the man. But art not thou thyself giddy with the fashion,
too, that thou hast shifted out of thy tale into telling me of
the fashion?   115

Borachio   Not so, neither. But know that I have tonight wooed Margaret,

Verges and Dogberry, 2012

Glossary

121 **possessed by** convinced by
137 **lock** hanging curl of hair known as a lovelock in Shakespeare's time
142 **goodly commodity** useful article
142 **taken up** arrested
143 **bills** long-handled, axe-headed tools
144 **in question** in demand

At the time

Using page 202, find out what Shakespeare's audience would have expected from a comedy. What were the differences between a comedy and a tragedy?

Activity 5: Exploring the structure of a comedy

a. In groups, decide who will play Conrad, Borachio and the First and Second Watchmen. Read aloud lines 133–144.

b. Using what you have found out in Act 3 Scene 3 about the characters and the situation, stage lines 133–144 in which the Watch arrest Borachio and Conrad.

c. Look back at the beginning of Act 3 Scene 3 where Dogberry gives advice to the Watch (pages 99–101). Why do you think the Watch ignore his advice and arrest Conrad and Borachio?

d. Act 3 Scene 3 is the first time in the play that we meet Dogberry, Verges and the Watch. It is just before the wedding and the audience knows that Claudio is planning to shame Hero on her wedding day. Discuss why you think Shakespeare decided to introduce the comic characters at this point in the action.

e. Write a paragraph explaining why you think Shakespeare put this scene in the play at this point in the action.

Did you know?

Shakespeare plays are often classified as 'comedies' or 'tragedies'. *Much Ado About Nothing* is classified as a comedy as the ending is considered to be a happy one, but there are things that happen in the play that are very serious for the characters involved. Some productions choose to emphasise the darker side of the play as opposed to treating it as pure comedy.

the Lady Hero's gentlewoman, by the name of Hero. She leans
me out at her mistress' chamber window, bids me a thousand
times good night. I tell this tale vilely, I should first tell thee how
the Prince, Claudio and my master, planted and placed and   120
possessed by my master Don John, saw afar off in the orchard
this amiable encounter.

Conrad   And thought they Margaret was Hero?

Borachio   Two of them did, the Prince and Claudio, but the devil my
master knew she was Margaret, and partly by his oaths, which   125
first possessed them, partly by the dark night, which did deceive
them, but chiefly by my villainy, which did confirm any slander
that Don John had made, away went Claudio enraged, swore
he would meet her as he was appointed next morning at the
temple, and there, before the whole congregation, shame her   130
with what he saw o'er night, and send her home again without
a husband.

First Watchman   We charge you, in the Prince's name. Stand.

Second Watchman   Call up the right Master Constable. We have here recovered the
most dangerous piece of lechery that ever was known in the   135
commonwealth.

First Watchman   And one Deformed is one of them. I know him, a wears a lock.

Conrad   Masters, masters.

Second Watchman   You'll be made bring Deformed forth, I warrant you.

Conrad   Masters—   140

First Watchman   Never speak, we charge you. Let us obey you to go with us.

Borachio   We are like to prove a goodly commodity, being taken up of
these men's bills.

Conrad   A commodity in question, I warrant you. Come, we'll obey you.

Exeunt

It is the day of the wedding. Hero sends Ursula to wake Beatrice and then discusses with Margaret what she will wear for her big day. Hero tells Margaret that her heart is heavy and Margaret urges her to look forward to the wedding night.

At the time

Using pages 204–205, find out about wedding fashions in Elizabethan England.

Hero and Margaret, 2014

Did you know?

The costume designer for an RSC production produces detailed drawings of what each character will wear. The costume designer first reads the script and picks up all the clues that are in it about the characters and the situation they are in. Then they consider the time period in which the production is set before producing their first drawings.

Activity 1: Exploring character and costume

a. In pairs, read aloud lines 5–18 with one of you as Margaret and the other as Hero.

b. Write design notes for Hero's wedding dress. Pay particular attention to what Margaret says in lines 14–18 about the Duchess of Milan's gown. The dress you design should be worth ten times more than this.

c. Look at line 19. Discuss and decide why you think Hero's heart is heavy. What is she worried about? Add Hero's worries to your design notes.

d. We know that Margaret has been a part of Borachio's plan to trick Claudio and Don Pedro the previous night by pretending to be Hero. Why do you think she does not tell Hero about her part in the trick?

Glossary

5 **Troth** in truth

5 **rebato** decorative collar

10 **tire** decorative headdress

13 **exceeds** beats all others

15 **cuts** slashes revealing even richer fabric underneath

15–16 **down sleeves** sleeves that are tight from elbow to wrist and fuller at the shoulder

16 **round underborne** worn over a petticoat

16–17 **bluish tinsel** blue silk cloth with silver or gold threads

23 **honourable** In the Book of Common Prayer, marriage is described as an honourable state

Act 3 | Scene 4

Enter Hero, Margaret and Ursula

Hero Good Ursula, wake my cousin Beatrice, and desire her to rise.

Ursula I will, lady.

Hero And bid her come hither.

Ursula Well.

Exit Ursula

Margaret Troth, I think your other rebato were better.   5

Hero No, pray thee, good Meg, I'll wear this.

Margaret By my troth, 's not so good and I warrant your cousin will say so.

Hero My cousin's a fool, and thou art another. I'll wear none but this.

Margaret I like the new tire within excellently, if the hair were a thought   10
browner. And your gown's a most rare fashion, i' faith. I saw the
Duchess of Milan's gown that they praise so.

Hero O, that exceeds, they say.

Margaret By my troth, 's but a night-gown in respect of yours: cloth
o' gold, and cuts, and laced with silver, set with pearls, down   15
sleeves, side sleeves, and skirts, round underborne with a bluish
tinsel. But for a fine, quaint, graceful, and excellent fashion,
yours is worth ten on't.

Hero God give me joy to wear it, for my heart is exceeding heavy.

Margaret 'Twill be heavier soon by the weight of a man.   20

Hero Fie upon thee, art not ashamed?

Margaret Of what, lady? Of speaking honourably? Is not marriage
honourable in a beggar? Is not your lord honourable without

Beatrice comes in, sounding as if she has a heavy cold, and reminds Hero that it is very nearly time for the wedding. Margaret challenges Beatrice to a battle of wits.

Hero and Margaret, 2012

Activity 2: Exploring the theme of male and female relationships

a. In groups, decide who will play Hero, Beatrice and Margaret. Read aloud lines 30–62.

b. Using the glossary boxes, put lines 30–62 into your own words.

c. Read aloud lines 30–62 again. This time, every time one of the characters feels they have scored a witty point against another character they should hit that character's script with their hand. For example, when Margaret says 'O illegitimate construction!' in line 38, she could hit Beatrice's script.

d. Discuss how the female characters speak and behave in this section. Who scores the most points and against whom and why? How do you think Margaret feels about Beatrice and why? How do you think Beatrice feels about Margaret and why? How do you think Hero feels about what is going on between her cousin and her maid?

e. Write a paragraph describing how Margaret, Beatrice and Hero behave during lines 30–62. Do you think they behave differently in this section than they do when the men in the play are present? Why do you think this is the case?

Glossary

25 **wrest** twist

30 **coz** cousin

34 **Clap's… love** let's sing a popular song that starts with rhythmic clapping

34 **burden** bass singing part for a male voice

37 **barns** bairns (children)

38 **illegitimate construction** false interpretation

40 **Hey-ho** sigh

41 **hawk… husband** A sigh is a call for all three things

42 **h** ache ('h' was pronounced 'aitch' in Shakespeare's time)

43 **turned Turk** changed faith

44 **the star** the Pole star, which is a navigational fixed point

45 **trow** I wonder

47 **gloves** These were often perfumed to disguise the smell of the leather

50–51 **professed apprehension** prided yourself on your wit

marriage? I think you would have me say 'saving your
reverence, a husband'. And bad thinking do not wrest true   25
speaking, I'll offend nobody. Is there any harm in 'the heavier
for a husband'? None, I think, and it be the right husband and
the right wife, otherwise 'tis light, and not heavy. Ask my Lady
Beatrice else, here she comes.

Enter Beatrice

Hero Good morrow, coz.   30

Beatrice Good morrow, sweet Hero.

Hero Why how now? Do you speak in the sick tune?

Beatrice I am out of all other tune, methinks.

Margaret Clap's into 'Light o' love'. That goes without a burden. Do you
sing it and I'll dance it.   35

Beatrice Ye light o' love, with your heels. Then if your husband have
stables enough, you'll see he shall lack no barns.

Margaret O illegitimate construction! I scorn that with my heels.

Beatrice 'Tis almost five o'clock, cousin. 'Tis time you were ready. By my
troth, I am exceeding ill. Hey-ho.   40

Margaret For a hawk, a horse, or a husband?

Beatrice For the letter that begins them all: h.

Margaret Well, and you be not turned Turk, there's no more sailing by
the star.

Beatrice What means the fool, trow?   45

Margaret Nothing, I. But God send everyone their heart's desire.

Hero These gloves the Count sent me, they are an excellent perfume.

Beatrice I am stuffed, cousin. I cannot smell.

Margaret A maid, and stuffed! There's goodly catching of cold.

Beatrice O God help me, God help me. How long have you professed   50
apprehension?

Margaret says she wouldn't dare to think that Beatrice is in love, but mentions that Benedick has grown up and accepted that he may marry. Ursula returns with the news that Don Pedro, Claudio, Benedick, Don John and all the gentlemen of the town have come to take Hero to church.

Margaret, Beatrice and Hero, 2012

Did you know?

The meaning of the words in a play depends on the way in which the actors speak them. **Tone**, **emphasis**, volume and **pace** are as important as the dictionary definition of the words in terms of conveying meaning.

Key terms

Tone as in 'tone of voice'; expressing an attitude through how you say something

Emphasis stress given to words when speaking

Pace the speed at which someone speaks

Subtext the underlying meaning in the script

Activity 3: Exploring subtext

a. In pairs, read aloud lines 60–70, swapping readers at the punctuation marks.

b. Now decide who will play Margaret and Beatrice. The person playing Margaret reads lines 60–70 while the person playing Beatrice listens politely, nodding and smiling to encourage Margaret.

c. Now the person playing Margaret should read lines 60–70 again, but this time the person playing Beatrice can interrupt Margaret with comments and questions at any time, and say what Beatrice is thinking when she hears Margaret's words. The person playing Margaret should try not to be put off by these interruptions.

d. Write a character profile for Margaret based on what you have discovered about her in Act 3 Scene 4, using evidence from the play in your work.

Glossary

53 **in your cap** a fool wore a special cap

55 **carduus benedictus** holy thistle, a herbal remedy

56 **qualm** nausea

62 **by'r Lady** by Our Lady

62 **list** please

72 **Not… gallop** nothing that's not true

Margaret Ever since you left it. Doth not my wit become me rarely?

Beatrice It is not seen enough, you should wear it in your cap. By my
troth, I am sick.

Margaret Get you some of this distilled *carduus benedictus* and lay it to   55
your heart. It is the only thing for a qualm.

Hero There thou prick'st her with a thistle.

Beatrice *Benedictus*, why *benedictus*? You have some moral in this
benedictus.

Margaret Moral? No, by my troth, I have no moral meaning. I meant,   60
plain holy-thistle. You may think perchance that I think you are
in love. Nay, by'r Lady, I am not such a fool to think what I list,
nor I list not to think what I can, nor indeed I cannot think, if
I would think my heart out of thinking, that you are in love, or
that you will be in love, or that you can be in love. Yet Benedick   65
was such another, and now is he become a man. He swore he
would never marry, and yet now in despite of his heart he eats
his meat without grudging. And how you may be converted
I know not, but methinks you look with your eyes, as other
women do.   70

Beatrice What pace is this that thy tongue keeps?

Margaret Not a false gallop.

Enter Ursula

Ursula Madam, withdraw. The Prince, the Count, Signor Benedick,
Don John and all the gallants of the town are come to fetch you
to church.   75

Hero Help to dress me, good coz, good Meg, good Ursula.

Exeunt

113

Dogberry and Verges visit Leonato in order to report Borachio and Conrad's arrest, but they do not speak directly. Leonato is very busy getting ready for the wedding and tries in vain to find out what they have come to say.

Dogberry, Verges and Leonato, 2006

Activity 1: Exploring stage business

a. In groups, decide who will play Leonato, Dogberry and Verges. Read aloud lines 1–34.

b. Stand up and read lines 1–34 again. This time, read the lines as if Dogberry and Verges are on Leonato's doorstep and he is patiently trying to find out what they have to say.

c. Now imagine that Leonato is getting ready for the wedding. Think of something he could be doing on the wedding morning, which is pulling his attention away from Dogberry and Verges. For example, he could be trying to tie his bow tie neatly. Read lines 1–34 again, this time as if Leonato is far more interested in whatever activity he is engaged in to get ready for the wedding than in what Dogberry and Verges have to say.

d. Which interpretation of this scene do you prefer from tasks b and c? Explain your reasons.

Key term

Stage business activity onstage

Glossary

2 **confidence** confidential chat

2 **decerns** This is a malapropism for 'concerns'

10 **honest… brows** This was a proverbial saying

13 **odorous** This is a malapropism for 'odious'

13 **Palabras** Spanish for 'words' (short for the saying 'pocas palabras', which means 'few words')

16 **tedious** This is a malapropism for 'generous'

25 **arrant knaves** utter villains

Act 3 | Scene 5

Enter Leonato, Dogberry and Verges

Leonato What would you with me, honest neighbour?

Dogberry Marry, sir, I would have some confidence with you that decerns you nearly.

Leonato Brief, I pray you, for you see it is a busy time with me.

Dogberry Marry, this it is, sir.   5

Verges Yes, in truth it is, sir.

Leonato What is it, my good friends?

Dogberry Goodman Verges, sir, speaks a little off the matter, an old man, sir, and his wits are not so blunt as, God help, I would desire they were, but in faith, honest as the skin between his brows.   10

Verges Yes, I thank God, I am as honest as any man living that is an old man and no honester than I.

Dogberry Comparisons are odorous. Palabras, neighbour Verges.

Leonato Neighbours, you are tedious.

Dogberry It pleases your worship to say so, but we are the poor duke's   15
officers. But truly, for mine own part, if I were as tedious as a
king I could find it in my heart to bestow it all of your worship.

Leonato All thy tediousness on me, ah?

Dogberry Yea, and 'twere a thousand pound more than 'tis, for I hear as
good exclamation on your worship as of any man in the city,   20
and though I be but a poor man, I am glad to hear it.

Verges And so am I.

Leonato I would fain know what you have to say.

Verges Marry, sir, our watch tonight, excepting your worship's presence,
ha' ta'en a couple of as arrant knaves as any in Messina.   25

When Dogberry finally gets round to telling Leonato that the Watch have arrested two suspicious people, Leonato asks them to deal with it themselves. Leonato leaves for the wedding, and Dogberry and Verges get ready to cross-examine Borachio and Conrad.

Activity 2: Exploring a comic scene

a. Look at the photo on this page of the 2014 RSC production. Which line from lines 34–41 do you think is being spoken in this photo? Explain your reasons.

b. Look back over Act 3 Scene 5. Write two sentences: the first should explain why you think Dogberry and Verges do not get around to explaining the details of the arrest; the second should explain how what happens in Act 3 Scene 5 helps to create **dramatic tension**.

Key term

Dramatic tension the anticipation of an outcome on stage, keeping the audience in suspense

Leonato, a servant, Dogberry and Verges, 2014

Dogberry A good old man, sir. He will be talking. As they say, 'When the age is in, the wit is out'. God help us, it is a world to see. Well said, i' faith, neighbour Verges. Well, God's a good man. And two men ride of a horse, one must ride behind. An honest soul, i'faith, sir, by my troth he is, as ever broke bread. But, God is to   30 be worshipped, all men are not alike, alas, good neighbour.

Leonato Indeed, neighbour, he comes too short of you.

Dogberry Gifts that God gives.

Leonato I must leave you.

Dogberry One word, sir, our watch, sir, have indeed comprehended two   35 auspicious persons and we would have them this morning examined before your worship.

Leonato Take their examination yourself, and bring it me. I am now in great haste, as it may appear unto you.

Dogberry It shall be suffigance.   40

Leonato Drink some wine ere you go. Fare you well.

Enter a Messenger

Messenger My lord, they stay for you to give your daughter to her husband.

Leonato I'll wait upon them, I am ready.

Exeunt Leonato and Messenger

Dogberry Go, good partner, go get you to Francis Seacole, bid him bring   45 his pen and inkhorn to the jail. We are now to examination these men.

Verges And we must do it wisely.

Dogberry We will spare for no wit, I warrant you. Here's that shall drive some of them to a non-come. Only get the learned writer to set   50 down our excommunication and meet me at the jail.

Exeunt

Exploring Act 3

Activity 1: Preparing for a big scene

a. In groups, look back over Act 3 and each choose one of the characters. Imagine it is just before the wedding and the characters you have chosen in your groups are in the final moments of getting ready for the event. Create a freeze-frame that shows that final moment.

b. Bring your freeze-frame to life as each character speaks their greatest hope for the wedding in their own words. Repeat this exercise, but this time with each character speaking their greatest fear.

c. Write a list of three hopes and three fears for the character you have chosen in that final moment.

d. Join with another group and share your work.

e. Write two or three paragraphs that explain how Act 3 sets up audience expectations for the wedding. Use evidence from the play in your explanation.

Beatrice, Ursula and Hero, 2006

Activity 2: Exploring the development of themes

a. In groups, look back over Act 3 and each choose one of the
   following themes:
   - love and marriage
   - male and female relationships
   - deception
   - loyalty
   - honour.
b. Trace how ideas about your chosen theme have been
   developed in Act 3. Discuss your ideas and rank the
   themes in order of their importance in this act.
c. Prepare a presentation about your chosen theme.

The wedding party assembles and the ceremony begins. Friar Francis asks if Claudio or Hero know of any reason why they should not be married. In front of everyone, Claudio asks Leonato if his daughter is a virgin.

Leonato, the Friar, Beatrice, Hero, Claudio and Don Pedro, 2012

Activity 1: Exploring an entrance

a. Go through the list of characters on page 11 and decide who you think would be at the wedding. Start with the list under the **stage direction** 'Enter' on page 121. In many productions, other characters such as Hero's uncle Antonio are also included. You can include whoever you like as long as you have a clear reason for why the character would attend the wedding.

b. Imagine the entrance of the wedding party. Put the characters in the order of who you think should enter first, second and so on, until everyone is assembled.

c. Write a sentence for each character explaining why you think they should enter at that point in the sequence. Your sentence should include what the character's attitude to the event is, an activity they would be doing as they enter and an **adjective** to describe their behaviour.

Glossary

1 **plain form** simplest formalities
9 **impediment** barrier
10 **conjoined** united
17 **Interjections** spoken words full of sudden or strong feeling
17–18 **Why then... ha he** Benedick quotes a standard school grammar book
21 **maid** virgin

Key terms

Stage direction an instruction in the text of a play, e.g. indicating which characters enter and exit a scene
Adjective a word that describes a noun, e.g. *blue, happy, big*

Act 4 | Scene 1

Enter Don Pedro, Don John, Leonato, Friar Francis, Claudio, Benedick, Hero and Beatrice

Leonato Come, Friar Francis, be brief. Only to the plain form of marriage, and you shall recount their particular duties afterwards.

Friar You come hither, my lord, to marry this lady?

Claudio No. 5

Leonato To be married to her. Friar, you come to marry her.

Friar Lady, you come hither to be married to this count?

Hero I do.

Friar If either of you know any inward impediment why you should not be conjoined, I charge you on your souls to utter it. 10

Claudio Know you any, Hero?

Hero None, my lord.

Friar Know you any, Count?

Leonato I dare make his answer: none.

Claudio O what men dare do! What men may do! What men daily do, 15
not knowing what they do!

Benedick How now! Interjections? Why then, some be of laughing, as ah, ha he!

Claudio Stand thee by, Friar. Father, by your leave,
Will you with free and unconstrainèd soul 20
Give me this maid, your daughter?

Leonato As freely, son, as God did give her me.

Claudio criticises Hero in front of the whole congregation, accusing her of being a lustful woman, unfit to be his wife. He says he can prove it and that therefore he will not marry her. Leonato is confused.

Benedick, Claudio, the Friar and Hero, 2014

Activity 2: Exploring language and character

a. In small groups, look at page 123 and write a list of all the phrases that Claudio uses to describe Hero. For example, you might select 'rotten orange' in line 28.

b. Using the glossary, **paraphrase** each phrase on your list.

c. Decide who will play Hero. This person should sit on a chair between two other people, who should be close enough to whisper into Hero's ear. The person on the left should whisper the phrases Claudio uses on page 123. At the same time, the person on the right should whisper your paraphrases of these.

d. Swap roles so that each of you has the opportunity to listen as if you are Hero, to whisper Claudio's words and to whisper your paraphrases.

e. Discuss which words had the most powerful effect on you as you listened in role as Hero. Decide which words might be being spoken in the photo on this page. Give reasons for your suggestion.

f. Write a paragraph that explains the effect of Claudio's words on Hero.

Glossary

24 **counterpoise** equally balance
26 **learn** teach
29 **semblance** false appearance
34 **witness** give evidence of
37 **luxurious** lustful
40 **approvèd wanton** proven promiscuous person
44 **known** had intercourse with
48 **word too large** improper suggestion
52 **Out on** that's enough of
52 **write against** denounce
53 **Dian** virgin goddess of the moon
54 **blown** fully opened

Key term

Paraphrase put a line or section of text into your own words

Claudio	And what have I to give you back whose worth May counterpoise this rich and precious gift?
Don Pedro	Nothing, unless you render her again.
Claudio	Sweet Prince, you learn me noble thankfulness. There, Leonato, take her back again. Give not this rotten orange to your friend. She's but the sign and semblance of her honour. Behold how like a maid she blushes here! O, what authority and show of truth Can cunning sin cover itself withal! Comes not that blood as modest evidence To witness simple virtue? Would you not swear, All you that see her, that she were a maid, By these exterior shows? But she is none. She knows the heat of a luxurious bed. Her blush is guiltiness, not modesty.
Leonato	What do you mean, my lord?
Claudio	Not to be married, Not to knit my soul to an approvèd wanton.
Leonato	Dear my lord, if you, in your own proof Have vanquished the resistance of her youth And made defeat of her virginity—
Claudio	I know what you would say. If I have known her, You will say she did embrace me as a husband, And so extenuate the forehand sin. No, Leonato, I never tempted her with word too large, But as a brother to his sister, showed Bashful sincerity and comely love.
Hero	And seemed I ever otherwise to you?
Claudio	Out on thee, seeming, I will write against it. You seem to me as Dian in her orb, As chaste as is the bud ere it be blown.

Line numbers: 25, 30, 35, 40, 45, 50

Leonato appeals to Don Pedro, who says that Hero's actions have dishonoured him because he wooed her on Claudio's behalf. Leonato urges his daughter to tell the truth. Claudio asks her for the identity of the man she talked with on the previous night at her bedroom window.

Claudio and Hero, 2006

Activity 3: Exploring the character of Hero

a. In groups, decide who will play Claudio, Leonato, Hero and Don Pedro (who remains silent). Read aloud lines 66–78.

b. Stand in a square, a few steps apart. To help you understand more about the characters, their relationships and their motives, read lines 66–78 again. This time, as you speak and listen, you should keep choosing between the following movements:
   - Take a step towards another character.
   - Take a step away from another character.
   - Turn towards another character.
   - Turn away from another character.
   - Stand still.

   Try to make instinctive choices rather than planning what to do.

c. How would you describe the relationship between these characters?

d. Look back at page 38, when the same task is used to explore lines 15–25 of Act 2 Scene 1. In those lines, Hero did not speak. What do you think has changed for her that might make her speak out now? Until this point in the play, how has Hero spoken to her father? How has she spoken to Claudio? How and why has her behaviour changed?

Glossary

55 **intemperate** extreme

55 **blood** passion

56 **Venus** goddess of desire

56 **pampered animals** horses (believed by the Elizabethans to be sexually overactive)

58 **wide** off the mark

61 **stale** prostitute

64 **nuptial** wedding

75 **catechizing** Hero refers to being taught religious catechism, through question and answer, which begins, 'What is your name?'

76 **your name** Claudio refers to the names he has called her

	But you are more intemperate in your blood	55
	Than Venus or those pampered animals	
	That rage in savage sensuality.	

Hero Is my lord well that he doth speak so wide?

Leonato Sweet Prince, why speak not you?

Don Pedro   What should I speak?
I stand dishonoured, that have gone about   60
To link my dear friend to a common stale.

Leonato Are these things spoken, or do I but dream?

Don John Sir, they are spoken, and these things are true.

Benedick This looks not like a nuptial.

Hero 'True'. O God!   65

Claudio Leonato, stand I here?
Is this the Prince? Is this the Prince's brother?
Is this face Hero's? Are our eyes our own?

Leonato All this is so. But what of this, my lord?

Claudio Let me but move one question to your daughter,   70
And by that fatherly and kindly power
That you have in her, bid her answer truly.

Leonato I charge thee do so, as thou art my child.

Hero O, God defend me, how am I beset.
What kind of catechizing call you this?   75

Claudio To make you answer truly to your name.

Hero Is it not Hero? Who can blot that name
With any just reproach?

Claudio   Marry, that can Hero.
Hero itself can blot out Hero's virtue.
What man was he talked with you yesternight   80
Out at your window betwixt twelve and one?
Now if you are a maid, answer to this.

Hero denies that she met a man at her bedroom window, but Don Pedro and Claudio take her denial as proof that she is lying because they witnessed it. Borachio has confessed that he has been with Hero secretly many times. Leonato wishes he was dead and Hero falls to the ground as if dead. Don John takes his brother and Claudio away, while Beatrice appeals for someone to help her cousin.

Beatrice and Hero, 2012

Activity 4: Exploring the theme of male and female relationships

a. In groups, decide who will play Don Pedro, Don John, Claudio and Leonato. Read aloud lines 85–105.

b. Discuss Hero's situation. Has Hero done what Claudio, Don Pedro and Don John are accusing her of? Why do you think Leonato says line 105? How would you feel if you were Hero? Why do you think Hero falls to the ground? How do you think Claudio would react to this happening? Give reasons for your answers.

c. Create a **freeze-frame** showing what you think is the most important moment in the action on page 127.

d. Choose a line or phrase from page 127 that would go with your freeze-frame. Explain why you chose that line or phrase.

e. Write a paragraph explaining how Hero is treated on page 127 and what this treatment shows about the **theme** of male and female relationships in the play.

Glossary

95 **misgovernment** misconduct
101 **gates of love** the senses, especially the eyes
102 **conjecture** suspicion
108 **spirits** life force

Key terms

Freeze-frame a physical, still image created by people to represent an object, place, person or feeling

Theme the main ideas explored in a piece of literature, e.g. the themes of love and marriage, male and female relationships, deception, loyalty and honour might be considered key themes of *Much Ado About Nothing*

Hero   I talked with no man at that hour, my lord.

Don Pedro   Why, then are you no maiden. Leonato,
I am sorry you must hear. Upon mine honour,   85
Myself, my brother and this grievèd Count
Did see her, hear her, at that hour last night
Talk with a ruffian at her chamber-window,
Who hath indeed, most like a liberal villain,
Confessed the vile encounters they have had   90
A thousand times in secret.

Don John   Fie, fie, they are
Not to be named, my lord, not to be spoke of.
There is not chastity enough in language
Without offence to utter them. Thus, pretty lady,
I am sorry for thy much misgovernment.   95

Claudio   O Hero! What a Hero hadst thou been
If half thy outward graces had been placed
About thy thoughts and counsels of thy heart?
But fare thee well, most foul, most fair, farewell.
Thou pure impiety and impious purity.   100
For thee I'll lock up all the gates of love,
And on my eyelids shall conjecture hang
To turn all beauty into thoughts of harm,
And never shall it more be gracious.

Leonato   Hath no man's dagger here a point for me?   105

Hero falls to the ground

Beatrice   Why, how now, cousin, wherefore sink you down?

Don John   Come. Let us go. These things come thus to light
Smother her spirits up.

Exeunt Don Pedro, Don John and Claudio

Benedick   How doth the lady?

Beatrice   Dead, I think. Help, uncle!
Hero, why Hero! Uncle! Signor Benedick! Friar!   110

Hero revives and is comforted by Beatrice and Friar Francis. Leonato wishes his daughter had died to cover the shame that she has brought upon him.

Leonato, 2006

Glossary

115 **look up** revive, or look to heaven for help

119 **printed in her blood** shown in her blushes, or now stamped on her life

123 **on the rearward of** immediately after

125 **frame** plan

129 **issue** child

130 **mired** stuck in deep mud

141 **attired** dressed

Activity 5: Exploring the language of relationships

a. In pairs, read aloud Leonato's speech from lines 117–140, swapping readers at the punctuation marks.

b. Discuss what Leonato's use of 'thou' reveals about his relationship with his daughter. Look at the 'Did you know?' box to help you.

c. Read lines 117–140 again, swapping at the punctuation marks. This time, emphasise the **pronouns** by pointing to yourself when you say 'I', 'my', 'mine' or 'myself', pointing to your partner when you say 'thine', 'thy' or 'thou' and pointing to an imaginary other at your side when you say 'her' or 'she'. How does this change your understanding of the speech?

d. In your pairs, imagine you are both Leonato. One of you should write a letter to Don Pedro, explaining how you feel in lines 117–140. The other person should write a letter to Hero, explaining how you feel in lines 117–140. Use words from lines 117–140 in your letter.

e. Swap letters and consider the differences in how Leonato talks about his daughter and expresses his feelings, depending on who he is communicating with.

Key term

Pronoun a word (such as I, he, she, you, it, we or they) that is used instead of a noun

Did you know?

In Shakespeare's time, people used 'thou' instead of 'you' for people they were close to. The actors at the RSC explore which form of address their characters use because it is a clue that helps the actors to understand the nature of their characters' relationships.

Leonato   O fate! Take not away thy heavy hand.
Death is the fairest cover for her shame
That may be wished for.

Beatrice   How now, cousin Hero?

Friar   Have comfort, lady.

Leonato   Dost thou look up?   115

Friar   Yea, wherefore should she not?

Leonato   Wherefore? Why, doth not every earthly thing
Cry shame upon her? Could she here deny
The story that is printed in her blood?
Do not live, Hero, do not ope thine eyes,   120
For did I think thou wouldst not quickly die,
Thought I thy spirits were stronger than thy shames,
Myself would on the rearward of reproaches
Strike at thy life. Grieved I, I had but one?
Chid I for that at frugal nature's frame?   125
O one too much by thee. Why had I one?
Why ever wast thou lovely in my eyes?
Why had I not with charitable hand
Took up a beggar's issue at my gates,
Who smearèd thus and mired with infamy,   130
I might have said, 'No part of it is mine,
This shame derives itself from unknown loins.'
But mine, and mine I loved, and mine I praised
And mine that I was proud on, mine so much
That I myself was to myself not mine   135
Valuing of her. Why she, O she is fallen
Into a pit of ink, that the wide sea
Hath drops too few to wash her clean again,
And salt too little which may season give
To her foul-tainted flesh.

Benedick   Sir, sir, be patient.   140
For my part, I am so attired in wonder,
I know not what to say.

The Friar protests Hero's innocence. Leonato refuses to listen to the Friar's reasoning.

The Friar, 2014

Glossary

144 **bedfellow** It was usual for two adults of the same
   gender to share a bed in Elizabethan England
161 **her maiden truth** the truth of her virginity
163 **experimental seal** life experience
163–164 **warrant... book** confirm what I have researched
170 **perjury** lying under oath

Did you know?

If lines contain a lots of vowel sounds, it can indicate stronger emotions. As an exercise in the rehearsal room, actors sometimes speak aloud just the vowel sounds to help them connect to the emotion the character feels. For example, think about the sounds you make when you're watching a fireworks display or are in pain or shouting for help. We rely heavily on vowel sounds to convey emotion and feeling.

Activity 6: Exploring the emotional impact of language

a. In pairs, read aloud Leonato's speech from lines 147–151, swapping readers at the punctuation marks.
b. Read the speech in the same way again, but this time emphasise and exaggerate the **vowel** sounds in the words.
c. Which repeated sound can you hear most clearly? Discuss what strong emotion Leonato might be expressing with this sound.
d. Leonato believes Claudio, Don Pedro and Don John rather than listening to his daughter. In what ways might his feelings be guiding his judgement?
e. Read lines 152–167 where Friar Francis notes the detail of Hero's reactions to the accusations that have been made against her. Pick out two details that he notes as proof of her innocence.
f. Which key emotions do you think Leonato and Friar Francis show in lines 147–167? Write a paragraph or two explaining your answer, using evidence from these lines.

Beatrice   O, on my soul, my cousin is belied.

Benedick   Lady, were you her bedfellow last night?

Beatrice   No, truly not, although, until last night   145
             I have this twelvemonth been her bedfellow.

Leonato   Confirmed, confirmed. O, that is stronger made
             Which was before barred up with ribs of iron.
             Would the two princes lie, and Claudio lie,
             Who loved her so that, speaking of her foulness,   150
             Washed it with tears? Hence from her, let her die.

Friar   Hear me a little,
          For I have only been silent so long
          And given way unto this course of fortune
          By noting of the lady. I have marked   155
          A thousand blushing apparitions
          To start into her face; a thousand innocent shames
          In angel whiteness beat away those blushes.
          And in her eye there hath appeared a fire
          To burn the errors that these princes hold   160
          Against her maiden truth. Call me a fool,
          Trust not my reading nor my observations,
          Which with experimental seal doth warrant
          The tenor of my book; trust not my age,
          My reverence, calling, nor divinity,   165
          If this sweet lady lie not guiltless here
          Under some biting error.

Leonato   Friar, it cannot be.
             Thou seest that all the grace that she hath left
             Is that she will not add to her damnation
             A sin of perjury. She not denies it.   170
             Why seek'st thou then to cover with excuse
             That which appears in proper nakedness?

Friar   Lady, what man is he you are accused of?

Hero   They know that do accuse me. I know none.

Hero protests her innocence, so Benedick suggests that Don John is to blame for the misunderstanding. Leonato says he will confront Claudio and Don Pedro if they have wronged his daughter's honour. The Friar suggests that they tell everyone that Hero has actually died instead of simply fainting.

The Friar, Hero and Beatrice, 2014

Activity 7: Exploring language and sentence structure

a. In pairs, read aloud Leonato's speech from lines 187–197, swapping readers at the punctuation marks.

b. Read the speech again, this time swapping readers at the end of each line.

c. Now look at how many sentences there are in this speech. Why do you think the final sentence is so long? How fast do you have to speak to say it all in one breath?

d. What do you notice about line 197 (the last line of Leonato's speech and the first line of what Friar Francis says next)?

e. Read aloud the Friar's speech from lines 197–205, swapping readers at the punctuation marks. Note how many sentences there are.

f. Now read this speech aloud again, this time swapping readers at the end of each line.

g. Write a paragraph or two to explain why Friar Francis suggests that they pretend Hero is dead.

Glossary

179 **unmeet** improper
182 **misprision** misunderstanding
185 **John the bastard** This is the first time that any of the characters calls Don John this
186 **frame** design
191 **invention** resourcefulness
193 **reft** bereft
197 **quit... throughly** pay them back in full

If I know more of any man alive   175
Than that which maiden modesty doth warrant,
Let all my sins lack mercy. O my father,
Prove you that any man with me conversed
At hours unmeet, or that I yesternight
Maintained the change of words with any creature,   180
Refuse me, hate me, torture me to death.

Friar   There is some strange misprision in the Princes.

Benedick   Two of them have the very bent of honour.
And if their wisdoms be misled in this
The practise of it lives in John the bastard,   185
Whose spirits toil in frame of villainies.

Leonato   I know not. If they speak but truth of her
These hands shall tear her. If they wrong her honour
The proudest of them shall well hear of it.
Time hath not yet so dried this blood of mine,   190
Nor age so eat up my invention,
Nor fortune made such havoc of my means,
Nor my bad life reft me so much of friends,
But they shall find awaked in such a kind,
Both strength of limb and policy of mind,   195
Ability in means, and choice of friends,
To quit me of them throughly.

Friar   Pause awhile,
And let my counsel sway you in this case.
Your daughter here the Princes left for dead,
Let her awhile be secretly kept in,   200
And publish it that she is dead indeed.
Maintain a mourning ostentation
And on your family's old monument
Hang mournful epitaphs and do all rites
That appertain unto a burial.   205

Leonato   What shall become of this? What will this do?

Friar   Marry, this well carried shall on her behalf

Friar Francis proposes a plan to convince Claudio that Hero has really died of shame so that he will wish he had not accused her and her honour will be restored. He suggests that if things don't work out, Leonato can conceal Hero in a nunnery, away from the judgement of society.

The Friar and Leonato, 2012

Glossary

210 **travail** labour
214 **Of** by
217 **rack** stretch; exaggerate
223 **organ** part
224 **habit** clothing
228 **liver** The liver was thought to be where love was found in the body
232 **event** outcome
236 **wonder** gossip
239 **reclusive** solitary; withdrawn
242 **inwardness** heartfelt friendship

Activity 8: Exploring the Friar's plan

a. In pairs, read aloud lines 211–240, swapping readers at the punctuation marks.
b. Read the first sentence aloud and decide what you think are the most important words. Choose at least six words.
c. Create **gestures** that could go with each of the key words you have chosen. Use gestures that help you to express exactly what the character means.
d. Now read the sentence again, making the gestures.
e. Work through the rest of the speech in the same way.
f. Discuss the Friar's plan.
   i. Why do you think the Friar uses such detail in his plan?
   ii. How do the key words you have explored add to the impact of the Friar's speech?
   iii. In what ways do the ideas in the speech persuade Benedick and Leonato to accept the Friar's plan?
   iv. How does the Friar's plan develop your understanding of the theme of deception?

Did you know?

In Elizabethan times, the audience would say they were going to 'hear' rather than 'see' a play in the theatre. The audience was used to listening for prolonged periods of time.

Key term

Gesture a movement, often using the hands or head, to express a feeling or idea

Change slander to remorse, that is some good.
But not for that dream I on this strange course,
But on this travail look for greater birth.   210
She dying, as it must so be maintained,
Upon the instant that she was accused,
Shall be lamented, pitied, and excused
Of every hearer, for it so falls out
That what we have, we prize not to the worth   215
Whiles we enjoy it, but being lacked and lost,
Why then we rack the value, then we find
The virtue that possession would not show us
Whiles it was ours; so will it fare with Claudio.
When he shall hear she died upon his words,   220
Th'idea of her life shall sweetly creep
Into his study of imagination,
And every lovely organ of her life
Shall come apparelled in more precious habit,
More moving-delicate and full of life,   225
Into the eye and prospect of his soul
Than when she lived indeed. Then shall he mourn,
If ever love had interest in his liver,
And wish he had not so accusèd her.
No, though he thought his accusation true.   230
Let this be so, and doubt not but success
Will fashion the event in better shape
Than I can lay it down in likelihood.
But if all aim but this be levelled false,
The supposition of the lady's death   235
Will quench the wonder of her infamy.
And if it sort not well, you may conceal her,
As best befits her wounded reputation,
In some reclusive and religious life,
Out of all eyes, tongues, minds, and injuries.   240

Benedick Signor Leonato, let the Friar advise you.
And though you know my inwardness and love
Is very much unto the Prince and Claudio,

Leonato agrees to the Friar's plan. Benedick and Beatrice are left alone in the place where the wedding should have taken place. Beatrice is upset about what has happened and wants a man to challenge Claudio. Benedick and Beatrice declare their love for each other for the first time.

Beatrice, 2006

Activity 9: Exploring the theme of love

a. In pairs, standing back-to-back, read aloud lines 253–281 with one of you as Benedick and the other as Beatrice.

b. Read the lines again, this time face-to-face, but whisper the lines as if the characters do not want to be overheard.

c. Stand about five steps apart and read the lines again, loudly.

d. Discuss how these different ways of reading the lines change your understanding of the scene. How do you think Beatrice is speaking her line in the photo on this page? Explain your reasons.

e. The person playing Benedick should stand rooted to the spot. They are not allowed to move off that spot. Meanwhile, the person playing Beatrice should move wherever they like around Benedick. Read lines 253–281 again, using these rules.

f. Read the lines again, this time with Beatrice rooted to the spot and Benedick able to move wherever he likes around her. How does this change your understanding of the scene?

g. In role as Benedick or Beatrice, write a sentence that explains why your character declares their love for the other character during lines 253–281 and how they feel when they do. Swap sentences with your partner and discuss the differences between them.

Glossary

248 **twine** thread

250 **For... cure** desperate diseases need desperate cures (proverbial saying)

252 **prolonged** postponed

261 **even** direct

263 **office** task

270 **By my sword** Christians swore oaths on the hilt of a sword, which makes a cross shape

Did you know?

When actors first start to act out a scene they will often use different techniques or 'games' to explore it. For example, they might limit the amount of movement a character can make or the volume at which they can speak. Applying limitations to a scene in rehearsal can help actors to make discoveries about their characters and the situations they are in.

Yet, by mine honour, I will deal in this
As secretly and justly as your soul   245
Should with your body.

Leonato Being that I flow in grief,
The smallest twine may lead me.

Friar 'Tis well consented. Presently away,
For to strange sores strangely they strain the cure.   250
Come, lady, die to live. This wedding day
Perhaps is but prolonged. Have patience and endure.

Exeunt all but Benedick and Beatrice

Benedick Lady Beatrice, have you wept all this while?

Beatrice Yea, and I will weep a while longer.

Benedick I will not desire that.   255

Beatrice You have no reason; I do it freely.

Benedick Surely I do believe your fair cousin is wronged.

Beatrice Ah, how much might the man deserve of me that would
right her!

Benedick Is there any way to show such friendship?   260

Beatrice A very even way, but no such friend.

Benedick May a man do it?

Beatrice It is a man's office, but not yours.

Benedick I do love nothing in the world so well as you. Is not that
strange?   265

Beatrice As strange as the thing I know not. It were as possible for me to
say I loved nothing so well as you, but believe me not, and yet
I lie not. I confess nothing nor I deny nothing. I am sorry for
my cousin.

Benedick By my sword, Beatrice, thou lovest me.   270

Benedick says he will do anything for Beatrice, so she asks him to kill Claudio. Benedick says he will not and they argue. Beatrice wishes she were a man so that she could challenge Claudio.

Activity 10: Exploring obstacles

a. In pairs, read aloud lines 282–303 with one of you as Benedick and the other as Beatrice.

b. Join up with another pair and agree an **objective** for Beatrice. For example, an objective might be 'to escape from the situation'. Make sure you use all the clues in the text.

c. Decide who will play Beatrice and Benedick in your group. The other two members of your group should become physical barriers and attempt to stop Beatrice from leaving the scene. For example, imagine there is a door that Beatrice is trying to get out of. Read lines 282–303 again, following these rules. Benedick should try to stop Beatrice from leaving. Beatrice should try to achieve the agreed objective by any means possible. Nobody should touch anybody else.

d. Discuss what the **obstacles** are that prevent Beatrice from achieving her objective. Write a list of her obstacles.

e. Imagining you are Beatrice, write a letter to Benedick explaining why you ask him to kill Claudio. Use some of the words from lines 282–303 in your letter.

Glossary

271 **it** This refers to the oath or the sword

287 **I am... here** in my heart I am no longer here

297 **unmitigated rancour** total hostility

Key terms

Objective what a character wants to get or achieve in a scene, e.g. Beatrice wants to challenge Claudio

Obstacle what is in the way of a character getting what they want, e.g. Beatrice wants to challenge Claudio but can't because she is a woman

Did you know?

Actors at the RSC sometimes find it useful to speak their lines while trying to get past a physical barrier such as a table. This can help them to understand the obstacles that are preventing their character from achieving their objective.

Beatrice and Benedick, 2014

Beatrice Do not swear and eat it.

Benedick I will swear by it that you love me, and I will make him eat it
that says I love not you.

Beatrice Will you not eat your word?

Benedick With no sauce that can be devised to it. I protest I love thee.   275

Beatrice Why then, God forgive me.

Benedick What offence, sweet Beatrice?

Beatrice You have stayed me in a happy hour. I was about to protest
I loved you.

Benedick And do it with all thy heart.   280

Beatrice I love you with so much of my heart that none is left to protest.

Benedick Come, bid me do any thing for thee.

Beatrice Kill Claudio.

Benedick Ha, not for the wide world.

Beatrice You kill me to deny. Farewell.   285

Benedick Tarry, sweet Beatrice.

Beatrice I am gone though I am here. There is no love in you. Nay, I
pray you, let me go.

Benedick Beatrice.

Beatrice In faith, I will go.   290

Benedick We'll be friends first.

Beatrice You dare easier be friends with me than fight with mine enemy.

Benedick Is Claudio thine enemy?

Beatrice Is a not approved in the height a villain, that hath slandered,
scorned, dishonoured my kinswoman? O that I were a man!   295
What, bear her in hand until they come to take hands, and then
with public accusation, uncovered slander, unmitigated rancour?

Beatrice says that she wishes she were a man or that she knew a man who would challenge Claudio for slandering her cousin. Benedick agrees to do it.

Activity 11: Exploring the theme of honour

a. Look back at the 'At the time' on page 96, which explores the theme of honour. Discuss what the code of honour means to Benedick and Claudio, as soldiers, gentlemen and friends.

b. Write a list of all the reasons against Benedick challenging Claudio.

c. Discuss what happens in Act 4 Scene 1 and why the events of this scene might lead Benedick to question the traditional code of honour.

d. Write a list of all the reasons for Benedick challenging Claudio.

e. Look at line 317. By the end of Act 4 Scene 1, Benedick has agreed to challenge Claudio to a duel. Why do you think he does this? What do you think of Benedick's decision? Imagining you are Benedick, write a letter to Beatrice explaining why you agree to kill Claudio. Use words from Act 4 Scene 1 in your letter.

Glossary

301 **proper saying** likely story
306 **Count** This is triple **pun** where count could mean 'Claudio', 'account' and 'legal testimony'
306 **Comfit** a sweet covered and preserved in sugar
308 **valour into compliment** bravery into flattery
309 **turned into tongue** all talk
309 **trim** smooth
310 **Hercules** the strongest man (in mythology)
313 **Tarry** wait

Key term

Pun a play on words

Beatrice, 2014

	O God, that I were a man! I would eat his heart in the market place.
Benedick	Hear me, Beatrice.
Beatrice	Talk with a man out at a window – a proper saying!
Benedick	Nay but Beatrice—
Beatrice	Sweet Hero. She is wronged; she is slandered; she is undone.
Benedick	Beat—
Beatrice	Princes and counties! Surely, a princely testimony, a goodly Count Comfit, a sweet gallant, surely. O that I were a man for his sake! Or that I had any friend would be a man for my sake! But manhood is melted into curtsies, valour into compliment, and men are only turned into tongue, and trim ones too. He is now as valiant as Hercules that only tells a lie and swears it. I cannot be a man with wishing, therefore I will die a woman with grieving.
Benedick	Tarry, good Beatrice. By this hand, I love thee.
Beatrice	Use it for my love some other way than swearing by it.
Benedick	Think you in your soul the Count Claudio hath wronged Hero?
Beatrice	Yea, as sure as I have a thought or a soul.
Benedick	Enough, I am engaged. I will challenge him. I will kiss your hand, and so I leave you. By this hand, Claudio shall render me a dear account. As you hear of me, so think of me. Go comfort your cousin, I must say she is dead. And so, farewell.

Exeunt

Dogberry and Verges start their cross-examination of Borachio and Conrad, while the Sexton prepares to make a written record of the proceedings.

Activity 1: Exploring status

a. Look at the list of characters at the opening of Act 4 Scene 2. The Sexton can read and write, but Dogberry, Verges and the Watch cannot. Put the list of characters in order of richest to poorest, using your knowledge of the play so far.

b. In groups, read aloud lines 1–33. Who would you say was the most important character here? Who would you say was the least important? Give reasons for your suggestions.

c. In your groups, arrange yourselves into a status line with the characters in order of most important to least important.

d. Still on your feet, rearrange yourselves in order of who *thinks* they are the most important to who *thinks* they are the least important.

e. What were the differences between your status lines? Discuss whether those differences contribute to making Act 4 Scene 2 funny. Are we laughing at or laughing with the characters? Explain your thinking.

f. Write an account of the examination of the prisoners in lines 1–33 as if you are the Sexton. Make sure you include a record of Dogberry's **malapropisms** and explain how you felt about the proceedings.

Glossary

1 **dissembly** This is a malapropism for 'assembly'

5 **exhibition** This is a malapropism for 'commission'

11 **sirrah** 'sir' (spoken to social inferiors)

22–23 **go about with** get the better of

At the time

Using pages 200–201, find out how many people in the audience in Shakespeare's time could read and write. Was that more or less than we might expect today? How do you think people who could read and write were regarded by those who could not?

Key term

Malapropism mistaken use of a word that sounds like another word but has a very different meaning

Act 4 | Scene 2

Enter Dogberry, Verges, the Sexton, the Watch, Conrad and Borachio

Dogberry Is our whole dissembly appeared?

Verges O, a stool and a cushion for the sexton.

Sexton Which be the malefactors?

Dogberry Marry, that am I, and my partner.

Verges Nay, that's certain, we have the exhibition to examine.   5

Sexton But which are the offenders that are to be examined? Let them come before Master Constable.

Dogberry Yea, marry, let them come before me. What is your name, friend?

Borachio Borachio.   10

Dogberry Pray, write down 'Borachio'. Yours, sirrah?

Conrad I am a gentleman, sir, and my name is Conrad.

Dogberry Write down 'Master Gentleman Conrad'. Masters, do you serve God?

Conrad and Borachio Yea, sir, we hope.   15

Dogberry Write down, that they hope they serve God. And write 'God' first, for God defend but God should go before such villains. Masters, it is proved already that you are little better than false knaves and it will go near to be thought so shortly. How answer you for yourselves?   20

Conrad Marry, sir, we say we are none.

Dogberry A marvellous witty fellow, I assure you, but I will go about with him. Come you hither, sirrah. A word in your ear, sir, I say to you, it is thought you are false knaves.

The Watchmen testify what they saw and heard when they arrested Borachio and Conrad. The Sexton reveals that Don John secretly left Messina that morning. The Sexton also describes how Hero was accused and died at the wedding. Dogberry continues to misunderstand and threaten the prisoners, before binding them to take to Leonato's house.

Glossary

30 **eftest** quickest
42 **by mass** by the mass (mild swearing)

Dogberry, Conrad and Borachio, 2012

Activity 2: Exploring a comedic situation

a. Look back at pages 142–143 and remind yourself of the status relationships between the characters at the opening of Act 4 Scene 2.

b. In groups, decide who will play Dogberry, Borachio, Conrad, Verges, the Sexton and the First and Second Watchman. Read aloud lines 32–61.

c. Using chairs, set up the courtroom in which the examination of the prisoners takes place. Think carefully about who should be positioned where. Look at how the characters are positioned in the photo on this page.

d. Choose a line for each character from lines 32–61 with which you can bring your courtroom to life. Decide in what order you will speak your lines and how you will speak your lines to show an audience the status relationship between the characters.

e. Discuss what you think should happen moment by moment during lines 51–61.

f. Create freeze-frames for lines 53–54, 55, 57, 59–60 and 61. Make sure you include as much detail as you can and try to make each freeze-framed moment funny.

g. Imagining you are the Sexton, write a detailed report in modern English about the situation, for Leonato. Make use of the information in lines 32–54.

Borachio	Sir, I say to you we are none.	25
Dogberry	Well, stand aside. Fore God, they are both in a tale. Have you writ down, that they are none?	
Sexton	Master Constable, you go not the way to examine. You must call forth the watch that are their accusers.	
Dogberry	Yea, marry, that's the eftest way. Let the watch come forth. Masters, I charge you, in the Prince's name accuse these men.	30
First Watchman	This man said, sir, that Don John, the Prince's brother, was a villain.	
Dogberry	Write down 'Prince John a villain'. Why, this is flat perjury, to call a prince's brother villain.	35
Borachio	Master Constable—	
Dogberry	Pray thee, fellow, peace. I do not like thy look, I promise thee.	
Sexton	What heard you him say else?	
Second Watchman	Marry, that he had received a thousand ducats of Don John for accusing the Lady Hero wrongfully.	40
Dogberry	Flat burglary, as ever was committed.	
Verges	Yea, by mass, that it is.	
Sexton	What else, fellow?	
First Watchman	And that Count Claudio did mean, upon his words to disgrace Hero before the whole assembly, and not marry her.	45
Dogberry	O villain! Thou wilt be condemned into ever-lasting redemption for this.	
Sexton	What else?	
Second Watchman	This is all.	
Sexton	And this is more, masters, than you can deny. Prince John is this morning secretly stolen away. Hero was in this manner accused,	50

Conrad has called Dogberry an ass, which Dogberry denies. The prisoners are taken to Leonato's house.

Activity 3: Exploring a comic character

Look at the photo on this page, which shows an actor playing Dogberry in the 2006 RSC production.

a. Discuss and identify at least three things in the appearance of this actor that make him funny.

b. In what ways do the actor's costume and make-up enhance his appearance and add to the comic effect?

Glossary

55 **opinioned** pinioned; bound
57 **coxcomb** fool (whose hat looks like a cock's crest)
60 **varlet** servant; rascal
62 **suspect** This is a malapropism for 'respect'
69 **go to** I can tell you

Did you know?

In Shakespeare's company, there was an actor called Will Kemp who was famous for his comic characters. It is believed that Shakespeare wrote some characters, like Dogberry, especially for him.

Dogberry, 2006

in this very manner refused, and upon the grief of this suddenly died. Master Constable, let these men be bound and brought to Leonato's. I will go before and show him their examination.

Exit Sexton

Dogberry   Come, let them be opinioned.   55

Verges   Let them be in the hands—

Conrad   Off, coxcomb!

Dogberry   God's my life, where's the Sexton? Let him write down 'the Prince's officer coxcomb'. Come, bind them. Thou naughty varlet.   60

Conrad   Away! You are an ass, you are an ass.

Dogberry   Dost thou not suspect my place? Dost thou not suspect my years? O that he were here to write me down an ass! But masters, remember that I am an ass. Though it be not written down, yet forget not that I am an ass. No, thou villain, thou art   65
full of piety, as shall be proved upon thee by good witness. I am a wise fellow, and which is more, an officer, and which is more, a householder, and which is more, as pretty a piece of flesh as any is in Messina, and one that knows the law, go to, and a rich fellow enough, go to, and a fellow that hath had losses, and   70
one that hath two gowns and everything handsome about him. Bring him away. O that I had been writ down an ass!

Exeunt

Exploring Act 4

Activity 1: Exploring Act 4

Look back over Act 4, remembering all the events that have happened. In groups, imagine you are reviewers of a contemporary production of *Much Ado About Nothing*. Your job is to produce a detailed newspaper feature about Act 4 of the production.

- Plan your feature. You must include a headline and decide what the photo on the front page would be. You could make that photo by designing a freeze-frame and taking a digital photo of it. There should be a factual column relating what the events of Act 4 were, including quotations from Shakespeare's script. You could also include interviews with actors playing specific characters, the designer and the **director**. You could have a backstage gossip column. Include your own ideas to make your feature appealing to your readers.
- Divide up the writing of the various parts of the feature between the members of your group. You could work as individuals or in pairs.
- Meet regularly to review what you are doing.
- Finally, put your feature review together to share with the rest of your class.

Benedick, Claudio, Leonato, Hero, Antonio and Beatrice, 2014

Did you know?

Modern editions of Shakespeare's plays, like this one, divide the play up into five acts and then into scenes within each act. The five-act structure is useful for understanding the shape of the action. Usually the end of Act 3 or the beginning of Act 4 is the **dramatic climax** of the play, which is followed by **falling action**.

Activity 2: Exploring characters in Act 4

a. In groups, choose one of the following characters:
  - Leonato
  - Hero
  - Beatrice
  - Benedick.

  Look back over Act 4 and make a note of your chosen character's actions.

b. Discuss the ways in which your chosen character has been changed by the events of Act 4. Predict what you think will happen to this character in the final act of the play.

Antonio advises his brother to stop blaming himself for what has happened, but Leonato asserts that his grief is too strong to be controlled.

At the time

Using page 206, find out what sort of reasons there were for Elizabethans to formally challenge each other to a duel.

Leonato, 2006

Glossary

2 **second** assist
12 **every... for strain** with the same emotions, or musical tone
16 **wag** go away
16 **cry 'hem'** clear his throat
17 **Patch** mend
18 **candle-wasters** late-night drinkers
24 **preceptial** proverbial
25 **Fetter... thread** capture insanity in a flimsy thread
27 **office** business
29 **virtue** power
29 **sufficiency** ability

Key term

Monologue a long speech in which a character expresses their thoughts. Other characters may be present

Activity 1: Exploring the character of Leonato

a. In small groups, read aloud lines 8–26, swapping readers at the punctuation marks.

b. Two people read aloud lines 8–26, while the rest of the group should listen and echo out loud any words that have strong feelings in them. For example, you might echo 'joy' and 'overwhelmed' in line 9.

c. Discuss what state of mind Leonato is in, and why. What does his portrayal in the photo on this page suggest about his state of mind?

d. Imagine you are Leonato.
   i. Write down one word that describes what Leonato is feeling.
   ii. Write down one sentence in modern English that Leonato would like to say and who he would like to say it to (it could be any other character in the play, Hero's mother, God or anyone else you choose). For example, 'Don Pedro, why would you believe that my daughter would behave like that?'
   iii. Write down one thing in modern English that Leonato would like to do. For example, 'I wish I could turn back time'.

e. In pairs, compare your sentences and combine them in order to create a **monologue** that Leonato might speak.

Enter Leonato and Antonio

Antonio If you go on thus, you will kill yourself,
And 'tis not wisdom thus to second grief
Against yourself.

Leonato   I pray thee, cease thy counsel,
Which falls into mine ears as profitless
As water in a sieve. Give not me counsel,   5
Nor let no comforter delight mine ear
But such a one whose wrongs do suit with mine.
Bring me a father that so loved his child,
Whose joy of her is overwhelmed like mine,
And bid him speak of patience.   10
Measure his woe the length and breadth of mine,
And let it answer every strain for strain,
As thus for thus, and such a grief for such,
In every lineament, branch, shape, and form.
If such a one will smile and stroke his beard,   15
Bid sorrow wag, cry 'hem' when he should groan,
Patch grief with proverbs, make misfortune drunk
With candle-wasters, bring him yet to me,
And I of him will gather patience.
But there is no such man, for, brother, men   20
Can counsel and speak comfort to that grief
Which they themselves not feel, but tasting it,
Their counsel turns to passion, which before
Would give preceptial medicine to rage,
Fetter strong madness in a silken thread,   25
Charm ache with air and agony with words.
No, no, 'tis all men's office to speak patience
To those that wring under the load of sorrow,
But no man's virtue nor sufficiency
To be so moral when he shall endure   30

Leonato says that he will make Claudio, Don Pedro and all those who have dishonoured his daughter suffer. Don Pedro and Claudio, armed, hurry in and Leonato tells Claudio that he has done him wrong.

Leonato and Claudio, 2006

Did you know?

Shakespeare rarely uses **stage directions** in his scripts, but instead there are clues about the action of a scene in the **dialogue** between the characters. The actors at the RSC discover these clues in rehearsal and use them to inform their performance.

Activity 2: Exploring the action

a. In groups, decide who will play Antonio, Don Pedro, Claudio and Leonato. Read aloud lines 45–54. Note that the word 'hastily' in line 45 means that Don Pedro and Claudio have to enter as if they are on their way somewhere, in a hurry. Line 54 means that Claudio must have put his hand ready on his sword. These are action clues.

b. Discuss where you think lines 45–54 take place. We know that it is somewhere in Leonato's house or garden, but you can decide exactly where.

c. You are now going to agree the movements for these lines, known as **blocking**. On your feet, work out the blocking for lines 45–54, using all the action clues in the words. For example, if you think that Don Pedro and Claudio are coming out of a door from the house and down a path, decide where the door is and where the path is. Write notes on how you might stage lines 45–54, including the action clues.

Key terms

Stage direction an instruction in the text of a play, e.g. indicating which characters enter and exit a scene

Dialogue a discussion between two or more people

Blocking the movements agreed for **staging** a scene

Staging the process of selecting, adapting and developing the stage space in which a play will be performed

The like himself. Therefore give me no counsel,
My griefs cry louder than advertisement.

Antonio   Therein do men from children nothing differ.

Leonato   I pray thee, peace. I will be flesh and blood,
For there was never yet philosopher   35
That could endure the toothache patiently,
However they have writ the style of gods,
And made a push at chance and sufferance.

Antonio   Yet bend not all the harm upon yourself.
Make those that do offend you suffer too.   40

Leonato   There thou speak'st reason, nay I will do so.
My soul doth tell me Hero is belied,
And that shall Claudio know, so shall the Prince,
And all of them that thus dishonour her.

Enter Don Pedro and Claudio

Antonio   Here comes the Prince and Claudio hastily.   45

Don Pedro   Good den, good den.

Claudio   Good day to both of you.

Leonato   Hear you, my lords?

Don Pedro   We have some haste, Leonato.

Leonato   Some haste, my lord! Well, fare you well, my lord.
Are you so hasty now? Well, all is one.

Don Pedro   Nay, do not quarrel with us, good old man.   50

Antonio   If he could right himself with quarrelling,
Some of us would lie low.

Claudio   Who wrongs him?

Leonato   Marry thou dost wrong me, thou dissembler, thou.
Nay, never lay thy hand upon thy sword,
I fear thee not.

Leonato formally challenges Claudio to a duel, despite being an old man. Claudio refuses and Don Pedro supports him, but Leonato insists and Antonio joins his brother in the challenge.

Claudio, Antonio and Leonato, 2012

Activity 3: Exploring power through movement

a. In groups, decide who will play Leonato, Claudio, Don Pedro and Antonio. Read aloud lines 67–83.

b. Discuss the status of the characters here. Remember, status is made up of a combination of wealth, social and personal power. Which character has the highest rank? Which characters are the oldest and therefore most deserving of respect? Who is the host (who should be respected)?

c. Read the lines again, this time considering the status of the characters and how this would affect the action. Who is challenging whom in lines 67–83 and when specifically is this happening? How could you move to show that? Discuss how the status of the characters is suggested in the photo on this page.

d. Imagining you are Don Pedro, write a report in modern English describing what happens during lines 67–83.

Glossary

55 **beshrew** curse
58 **fleer** taunt
62 **head** face
66 **trial of a man** single combat
75 **nice fence** fancy swordsmanship
78 **doff me** put me off
82 **Win… wear me** if he beats me, then he can boast
84 **foining fence** a downward thrust in sword fighting

Claudio	Marry beshrew my hand	55
	If it should give your age such cause of fear.	
	In faith, my hand meant nothing to my sword.	

Leonato Tush, tush, man, never fleer and jest at me.
I speak not like a dotard nor a fool,
As under privilege of age to brag 60
What I have done being young, or what would do
Were I not old. Know, Claudio, to thy head,
Thou hast so wronged mine innocent child and me
That I am forced to lay my reverence by
And with grey hairs and bruise of many days, 65
Do challenge thee to trial of a man.
I say thou hast belied mine innocent child.
Thy slander hath gone through and through her heart,
And she lies buried with her ancestors,
O, in a tomb where never scandal slept, 70
Save this of hers, framed by thy villainy.

Claudio My villany?

Leonato   Thine, Claudio, thine, I say.

Don Pedro You say not right, old man.

Leonato   My lord, my lord,
I'll prove it on his body if he dare,
Despite his nice fence and his active practice, 75
His May of youth and bloom of lustihood.

Claudio Away, I will not have to do with you.

Leonato Canst thou so doff me? Thou hast killed my child.
If thou kill'st me, boy, thou shalt kill a man.

Antonio He shall kill two of us, and men indeed. 80
But that's no matter, let him kill one first.
Win me and wear me, let him answer me.
Come follow me, boy, come, sir boy, come follow me.
Sir boy, I'll whip you from your foining fence.
Nay, as I am a gentleman, I will. 85

Antonio insults Claudio at length, calling him a 'boy' and saying he is a liar. Leonato tries to intervene, but Antonio continues until Don Pedro refuses to hear the challenge on the grounds that the accusations against Hero were true and proven. Leonato and Antonio leave.

Activity 4: Exploring different interpretations through performance

a. In pairs, read lines 84–102 with one of you as Antonio and the other as Leonato.

b. Now read the lines again as if Antonio is genuinely very angry and Leonato is trying to calm him down.

c. Finally, read the lines as if Antonio is exaggerating in order to cover up the fact that Hero is not really dead and Leonato is trying to remind him not to over-exaggerate in case the others suspect that he is trying to trick them.

d. Discuss which version you prefer (the reading in either task b or c) and why. Which interpretation do you think the photo on this page shows?

e. Join up with another pair and decide who will play Antonio, Leonato, Don Pedro and Claudio. Read lines 84–102 aloud again. The people playing Don Pedro and Claudio should react, using **gestures** and verbal sounds to show their attitude to Antonio and Leonato.

f. Write a summary of lines 84–102 in modern English from the point of view of the character you have played.

g. Swap your summary with someone else in your group and pick out the differences between them. What does this suggest about what the different characters think and feel at this point in the play?

Leonato, 2014

Key term

Gesture a movement, often using the hands or head, to express a feeling or idea

Leonato Brother—

Antonio Content yourself. God knows, I loved my niece,
And she is dead, slandered to death by villains
That dare as well answer a man indeed
As I dare take a serpent by the tongue.   90
Boys, apes, braggarts, jacks, milksops.

Leonato Brother Antony—

Antonio Hold you content. What, man? I know them, yea,
And what they weigh, even to the utmost scruple.
Scambling, out-facing, fashion-monging boys,   95
That lie, and cog, and flout, deprave, and slander,
Go anticly, and show an outward hideousness,
And speak off half a dozen dangerous words,
How they might hurt their enemies, if they durst,
And this is all.   100

Leonato But, brother Antony—

Antonio   Come, 'tis no matter.
Do not you meddle, let me deal in this.

Don Pedro Gentlemen both, we will not wake your patience.
My heart is sorry for your daughter's death,
But on my honour she was charged with nothing   105
But what was true and very full of proof.

Leonato My lord, my lord—

Don Pedro   I will not hear you.

Leonato No? Come, brother, away. I will be heard.

Antonio And shall, or some of us will smart for it.

Exeunt Leonato and Antonio. Enter Benedick

Don Pedro See, see, here comes the man we went to seek.   110

Claudio Now, Signor, what news?

Benedick Good day, my lord.

enedick comes in and Claudio and Don Pedro tell him about what has just happened etween them, Leonato and Antonio. Benedick formally challenges Claudio.

Claudio, 2006

Activity 5: Exploring the theme of honour

a. In groups, decide who will play Claudio, Benedick and Don Pedro. Read aloud lines 120–141.

b. Stand in a triangle, a few steps apart. To help you understand more about the characters, their relationships and their motives, read lines 120–141 again. This time, as you speak and listen, you should keep choosing between the following movements:

- Take a step towards another character.
- Take a step away from another character.
- Turn towards another character.
- Turn away from another character.
- Stand still.

Try to make instinctive choices rather than planning what to do.

c. Look back at the discussions about honour on pages 96 and 140. Discuss what the code of honour means to Benedick, Claudio and Don Pedro, as soldiers, gentlemen and friends.

d. What do you think Benedick is feeling during lines 120–141? What do you think Claudio is trying to achieve and why is he behaving as he does? Why does Don Pedro start to refer to Benedick as 'he' rather than speaking directly to Benedick?

e. Imagining you are Benedick, write a letter to Don Pedro in modern English, using the idea of honour to explain the reasons for your actions in lines 120–141.

Glossary

114 **had like** were likely
114 **with** by
117 **doubt** suspect
120 **high-proof** in the height of
128 **care... cat** This is a proverbial warning against worrying too much
130 **in the career** in mid-gallop (in jousting, a sport where men rode towards each other carrying long poles called lances to try to knock each other off their horses)
132 **staff** lance
132 **broke cross** snapped in the middle
135 **how to... girdle** what he can do about it
138 **make it good** back up what I have said
139 **Do me right** accept my challenge

Key term

Theme the main ideas explored in a piece of literature, e.g. the themes of love and marriage, male and female relationships, deception, loyalty and honour might be considered key themes of *Much Ado About Nothing*

Don Pedro Welcome, signor. You are almost come to part almost a fray.

Claudio We had like to have had our two noses snapped off with two old
men without teeth. 115

Don Pedro Leonato and his brother. What think'st thou? Had we fought, I
doubt we should have been too young for them.

Benedick In a false quarrel there is no true valour. I came to seek you
both.

Claudio We have been up and down to seek thee, for we are high-proof 120
melancholy and would fain have it beaten away. Wilt thou use
thy wit?

Benedick It is in my scabbard. Shall I draw it?

Don Pedro Dost thou wear thy wit by thy side?

Claudio Never any did so, though very many have been beside their wit. 125
I will bid thee draw, as we do the minstrels, draw to pleasure us.

Don Pedro As I am an honest man, he looks pale. Art thou sick, or angry?

Claudio What, courage, man. What though care killed a cat, thou hast
mettle enough in thee to kill care.

Benedick Sir, I shall meet your wit in the career and you charge it against 130
me. I pray you choose another subject.

Claudio Nay, then, give him another staff. This last was broke cross.

Don Pedro By this light, he changes more and more. I think he be angry
indeed.

Claudio If he be, he knows how to turn his girdle. 135

Benedick Shall I speak a word in your ear?

Claudio God bless me from a challenge.

Benedick You are a villain. I jest not. I will make it good how you dare,
with what you dare, and when you dare. Do me right, or I will
protest your cowardice. You have killed a sweet lady and her 140
death shall fall heavy on you. Let me hear from you.

Don Pedro says that Beatrice told him that she could love Benedick dearly and that Hero confirmed that Beatrice loves Benedick. Benedick tells Don Pedro that he can no longer be in his company and reveals that Don John has run away from Messina, which is a clue that Hero was innocent.

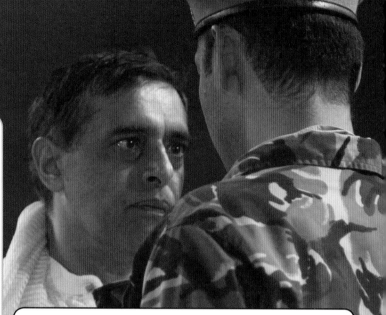

Benedick and Claudio, 2012

Glossary

142 **have good cheer** be entertained

144 **calf's head** fool

145 **capon** chicken

145 **curiously** skilfully

146 **naught** nothing

146 **woodcock** idiot

147 **ambles well** goes very slowly

153 **the tongues** foreign languages

158 **properest** most handsome

163–164 **God... garden** This recalls Adam, the first man, who tried to hide from God in the Garden of Eden

165 **horns** These are the sign of a cuckold (a married man whose wife commits adultery)

Key term

Freeze-frame a physical, still image created by people to represent an object, place, person or feeling

Activity 6: Exploring character

a. In groups, decide who will play Don Pedro, Claudio and Benedick. Read aloud lines 165–176.

b. Create a **freeze-frame** showing these characters as you think they would be in lines 165–166. This freeze-frame should show exactly what each character's attitude is at this moment.

c. Say what your character is thinking at lines 165–166.

d. Create a second freeze-frame showing Don Pedro, Claudio and Benedick in lines 174–176. This freeze-frame should show exactly what has changed in each character's attitude.

e. Say what your character is thinking at lines 174–176.

f. What moment is shown in the photo on this page? Explain your thinking.

g. Write a paragraph or two explaining what happens in lines 165–176. In your explanation, you should explore what changes in the attitude of the characters and why this is important.

Claudio   Well, I will meet you, so I may have good cheer.

Don Pedro   What, a feast, a feast?

Claudio   I' faith, I thank him. He hath bid me to a calf's head and a
capon, the which if I do not carve most curiously, say my knife's   145
naught. Shall I not find a woodcock too?

Benedick   Sir, your wit ambles well; it goes easily.

Don Pedro   I'll tell thee how Beatrice praised thy wit the other day. I said,
thou hadst a fine wit: 'True,' says she, 'a fine little one.' 'No,' said
I, 'a great wit.' 'Right,' says she, 'a great gross one.' 'Nay,' said   150
I, 'a good wit.' 'Just,' said she, 'it hurts nobody.' 'Nay,' said I, 'the
gentleman is wise.' 'Certain,' said she, 'a wise gentleman.' 'Nay,'
said I, 'he hath the tongues.' 'That I believe,' said she, 'for he
swore a thing to me on Monday night which he forswore on
Tuesday morning. There's a double tongue, there's two tongues.'   155
Thus did she, an hour together, trans-shape thy particular
virtues. Yet at last she concluded with a sigh thou wast the
properest man in Italy.

Claudio   For the which she wept heartily and said she cared not.

Don Pedro   Yea, that she did. But yet for all that, and if she did not hate him   160
deadly, she would love him dearly. The old man's daughter told
us all.

Claudio   All, all, and moreover, God saw him when he was hid in the
garden.

Don Pedro   But when shall we set the savage bull's horns on the sensible   165
Benedick's head?

Claudio   Yea, and text underneath, 'Here dwells Benedick the married
man'?

Benedick   Fare you well, boy, you know my mind. I will leave you now to
your gossip-like humour. You break jests as braggarts do their   170
blades, which God be thanked, hurt not. [To Don Pedro] My lord,
for your many courtesies I thank you. I must discontinue your
company. Your brother the bastard is fled from Messina.

Don Pedro and Claudio realise that Benedick's challenge is genuine. Dogberry, Verges and the Watch bring in their prisoners, Conrad and Borachio, but when Dogberry tries to explain what their offence is, Don Pedro cannot understand him.

Second Watchman, Borachio, Verges, Conrad and Dogberry, 2014

Activity 7: Exploring an offstage event

a. Read lines 186–187.

b. Imagine the scene in which Don John runs away from Messina. Shakespeare does not include this scene in his play, so we can decide what happens in it. Discuss your ideas about what might have happened. What was the exact moment at which Don John decided to leave Messina? What time of day was it? Why did he decide to go? How did he leave Messina?

c. In pairs or small groups, **improvise** the scene in which Don John leaves Messina. One of you play Don John and the others play any additional characters that you might need.

d. Discuss why you think Shakespeare has Don John leave Messina at this point in the action of the play.

e. Write a detailed recount of Don John leaving Messina.

Glossary

182 **goes in** wears
184–185 **He is… man** a man in love seems a hero to a fool, but the fool is wise compared to such a man
184 **doctor** wise person
186 **Pluck… sad** pull yourself together and be serious
189 **reasons** This word was pronounced 'raisins' in Shakespeare's time
189 **cursing** cursed
192 **Hearken after** enquire about

Key term

Improvise make up in the moment

Did you know?

Actors sometimes find it useful to improvise events that are mentioned or described in the play but not seen on stage, e.g. Don John's decision to leave Messina.

You have among you killed a sweet and innocent lady. For my
Lord Lackbeard there, he and I shall meet, and till then, peace   175
be with him.

Exit Benedick

Don Pedro He is in earnest.

Claudio In most profound earnest, and I'll warrant you, for the love of
Beatrice.

Don Pedro And hath challenged thee.   180

Claudio Most sincerely.

Don Pedro What a pretty thing man is when he goes in his doublet and
hose and leaves off his wit.

Enter Dogberry, Verges, the Watch, Conrad and Borachio

Claudio He is then a giant to an ape. But then is an ape a doctor to such
a man.   185

Don Pedro But soft you, let me be. Pluck up my heart and be sad. Did he
not say my brother was fled?

Dogberry Come you sir, if justice cannot tame you, she shall ne'er weigh
more reasons in her balance. Nay, and you be a cursing
hypocrite once, you must be looked to.   190

Don Pedro How now, two of my brother's men bound? Borachio one.

Claudio Hearken after their offence, my lord.

Don Pedro Officers, what offence have these men done?

Dogberry Marry sir, they have committed false report, moreover they have
spoken untruths, secondarily they are slanders, sixth and lastly   195
they have belied a lady, thirdly they have verified unjust things,
and to conclude, they are lying knaves.

Don Pedro First, I ask thee what they have done, thirdly I ask thee what's
their offence, sixth and lastly why they are committed, and to
conclude, what you lay to their charge.   200

Borachio confesses to Don Pedro and Count Claudio. They realise that Don John is a traitor and that Hero was innocent. Leonato, Antonio and the Sexton come in.

Borachio, 2012

Glossary

201 **in... division** with the argument clear

202 **one... suited** Between them, Dogberry and Don Pedro have presented one idea in six ways

204 **cunning** clever

225 **semblance** appearance

Key term

Paraphrase put a line or section of text into your own words

Activity 8: Exploring the effect of Borachio's speech

a. In small groups, read aloud lines 206–217, swapping readers at the punctuation marks.

b. **Paraphrase** Borachio's speech in lines 206–217.

c. Decide who will play Claudio. This person should sit on a chair between two other people, who should be close enough to whisper into Claudio's ear. The person on the left should whisper lines 206–217. At the same time, the person on the right should whisper their paraphrase of Borachio's speech.

d. Swap roles so that each of you has the opportunity to listen as if you are Claudio, to whisper Borachio's speech and to whisper your paraphrased lines.

e. Write a paragraph or two explaining the effects Borachio's words have on Claudio.

Claudio	Rightly reasoned, and in his own division. And by my troth there's one meaning well suited.
Don Pedro	Who have you offended, masters, that you are thus bound to your answer? This learned constable is too cunning to be understood. What's your offence?
Borachio	Sweet Prince, let me go no farther to mine answer. Do you hear me, and let this Count kill me. I have deceived even your very eyes. What your wisdoms could not discover, these shallow fools have brought to light, who in the night overheard me confessing to this man how Don John your brother incensed me to slander the Lady Hero, how you were brought into the orchard and saw me court Margaret in Hero's garments, how you disgraced her when you should marry her. My villainy they have upon record, which I had rather seal with my death than repeat over to my shame. The lady is dead upon mine and my master's false accusation, and briefly, I desire nothing but the reward of a villain.
Don Pedro	Runs not this speech like iron through your blood?
Claudio	I have drunk poison whiles he uttered it.
Don Pedro	But did my brother set thee on to this?
Borachio	Yea, and paid me richly for the practice of it.
Don Pedro	He is composed and framed of treachery And fled he is upon this villainy.
Claudio	Sweet Hero, now thy image doth appear In the rare semblance that I loved it first.
Dogberry	Come, bring away the plaintiffs. By this time our Sexton hath reformed Signor Leonato of the matter. And masters, do not forget to specify, when time and place shall serve, that I am an ass.
Verges	Here, here comes Master Signor Leonato, and the Sexton, too.

Enter Leonato, Antonio and the Sexton

205

210

215

220

225

230

Borachio claims that he alone was responsible for Hero's death, but Leonato accuses Claudio, Don Pedro and Don John. Claudio and Don Pedro ask Leonato to choose how he will take his revenge on them. Leonato asks Claudio to say something in memory of Hero at her tomb that night and then marry his 'niece'.

Borachio, Leonato and Conrad, 2014

Activity 9: Exploring dramatic irony

a. In pairs, read aloud lines 243–250 with one of you as Claudio and the other as Don Pedro.
b. These lines are in **iambic pentameter**. Clap the rhythm and say the words at the same time to remind yourself of it.
c. What does the audience know that Leonato knows, but Don Pedro and Claudio do not? How does this **dramatic irony** make the scene more effective?

Activity 10: Exploring the theme of honour

Look back at the discussions about honour on pages 96, 140 and 158. If you were Leonato, what would you ask Claudio and Don Pedro to do to satisfy the honour of your family?

Leonato Which is the villain? Let me see his eyes,
That when I note another man like him
I may avoid him. Which of these is he?

Borachio If you would know your wronger, look on me.

Leonato Art thou the slave that with thy breath hast killed   235
Mine innocent child?

Borachio   Yea, even I alone.

Leonato No, not so, villain, thou beliest thyself.
Here stand a pair of honourable men.
A third is fled, that had a hand in it.
I thank you, Princes, for my daughter's death.   240
Record it with your high and worthy deeds.
'Twas bravely done, if you bethink you of it.

Claudio I know not how to pray your patience,
Yet I must speak. Choose your revenge yourself,
Impose me to what penance your invention   245
Can lay upon my sin. Yet sinned I not
But in mistaking.

Don Pedro   By my soul, nor I.
And yet to satisfy this good old man,
I would bend under any heavy weight
That he'll enjoin me to.   250

Leonato I cannot bid you bid my daughter live,
That were impossible, but I pray you both
Possess the people in Messina here
How innocent she died, and if your love
Can labour ought in sad invention,   255
Hang her an epitaph upon her tomb
And sing it to her bones, sing it tonight.
Tomorrow morning come you to my house,
And since you could not be my son-in-law,
Be yet my nephew. My brother hath a daughter,   260
Almost the copy of my child that's dead,

Claudio agrees to speak in memory of Hero at her tomb and marry Leonato's 'niece'. Leonato thinks Margaret was involved in the scheme against Hero, but Borachio claims Margaret was innocent. Dogberry reminds Leonato that Conrad called him an ass and Leonato pays Dogberry.

Glossary

262 **she... of us** Leonato is pretending to have another niece
263 **right** legal right to be married
269 **naughty** wicked
271 **packed** involved
276 **under white and black** written down
279 **Deformed** Dogberry is confused. The Watch have heard 'what a deformed thief this fashion is' in line 99 of Act 3 Scene 3
288 **God... foundation** This was a phrase used by beggars
290 **arrant knave** complete rascal

Key term

Motivation a person's reason for doing something

Claudio and Leonato, 2012

Activity 11: Exploring Margaret's motivation

a. Read lines 269–275.
b. There are unanswered questions about why Margaret does what she does in *Much Ado About Nothing*. Using all the clues in the text, discuss the following questions:
   i. Do you think Margaret knew what she was doing when she put on Hero's clothes and answered Borachio as 'Hero' the night before Hero and Claudio's wedding?
   ii. Do you think Margaret knew why Claudio thought Hero had been having an affair with another man?
   iii. If she did know, why do you think she did not tell anyone?
c. Imagine the conversation that Margaret might have with Leonato. Write the script of this imagined conversation in modern English, using no more than ten lines.
d. In pairs, perform your script and give feedback to others. What have you learned about Margaret's **motivation** through this exploration?

And she alone is heir to both of us.
Give her the right you should have given her cousin,
And so dies my revenge.

Claudio   O noble sir!
Your over-kindness doth wring tears from me.   265
I do embrace your offer and dispose
For henceforth of poor Claudio.

Leonato Tomorrow then I will expect your coming.
Tonight I take my leave. This naughty man
Shall face to face be brought to Margaret,   270
Who I believe was packed in all this wrong,
Hired to it by your brother.

Borachio   No, by my soul, she was not,
Nor knew not what she did when she spoke to me,
But always hath been just and virtuous
In any thing that I do know by her.   275

Dogberry Moreover, sir, which indeed is not under white and black, this
plaintiff here, the offender, did call me 'ass'. I beseech you, let
it be remembered in his punishment. And also the watch heard
them talk of one Deformed. They say he wears a key in his ear
and a lock hanging by it, and borrows money in God's name,   280
the which he hath used so long and never paid that now men
grow hard-hearted and will lend nothing for God's sake. Pray
you, examine him upon that point.

Leonato I thank thee for thy care and honest pains.

Dogberry Your worship speaks like a most thankful and reverend youth,   285
and I praise God for you.

Leonato There's for thy pains.

Dogberry God save the foundation.

Leonato Go, I discharge thee of thy prisoner, and I thank thee.

Dogberry I leave an arrant knave with your worship, which I beseech   290
your worship to correct yourself for the example of others. God

Dogberry and Verges leave Borachio and Conrad in Leonato's custody. Don Pedro assures Leonato and Antonio that Claudio will marry Antonio's 'daughter' the next day. Claudio promises to mourn Hero at her tomb that night. Leonato instructs the Watch to bring the prisoners to talk with Margaret and find out the truth.

Claudio, the Watch, Verges, Borachio, Conrad, Leonato, the Sexton, Dogberry and Don Pedro, 2014

Activity 12: Exploring the theme of honour

a. Honour is a key theme in *Much Ado About Nothing*. The word 'honour' is still used today. In what ways has the meaning of the word 'honour' changed since Shakespeare wrote the play?

b. Write a letter to Hero as if you are either Don Pedro or Claudio, using the idea of honour to apologise for your actions. Use quotations from Act 5 Scene 1 in your letter. For example, you might use lines 105–106, lines 224–225 or any other relevant lines from the scene.

c. Swap your letter with a partner and discuss what you have written. Would you say Don Pedro and Claudio are honourable men? Explain your thinking.

Glossary

299 **lewd** crude or rude

At the time

Using page 207, explain what you have learned about what the word 'honour' meant to the Elizabethans.

keep your worship. I wish your worship well. God restore you to health. I humbly give you leave to depart, and if a merry meeting may be wished, God prohibit it. Come, neighbour.

Exeunt Dogberry and Verges

Leonato   Until tomorrow morning, lords, farewell.   295

Antonio   Farewell, my lords. We look for you tomorrow.

Don Pedro We will not fail.

Claudio   Tonight I'll mourn with Hero.

Leonato   [To the Watch] Bring you these fellows on. We'll talk with Margaret. How her acquaintance grew with this lewd fellow.

Exeunt

Benedick tries to persuade Margaret to help him write a love poem for Beatrice. Margaret teases him and then goes off to find Beatrice. Left alone, Benedick tries to sing a love song and struggles to find the words to draft his poem.

Margaret and Benedick, 2006

Activity 1: Exploring the theme of love

a. Read lines 21–30. As you read them, stand up on the first full stop, sit down on the next one and then continue standing up or sitting down every time you come to a full stop. If you come to a comma, stamp your foot.
b. What state of mind would you say Benedick was in?
c. What does Benedick's expression in the photo on this page suggest about his state of mind? Give reasons for your suggestion.
d. Write a paragraph or two explaining what you think Benedick's state of mind is during lines 21–30 and why he feels this way.

Glossary

4–5 **come over** surpass
6–7 **keep below stairs** remain a servant who works downstairs
8 **catches** picks things up quickly
9 **fencer's foils** blunted swords used for practice
11 **give... bucklers** throw down my shield
13 **put in... vice** fit the buckler with a screw-in spike
21 **Leander** In Greek mythology, Leander swam every night across the river that separated him from his love, Hero
22 **Troilus** In mythology, Troilus was introduced to his true love Cressida by her uncle Pandarus
23 **quondam carpet-mongers** ladies' men from past times

Act 5 | Scene 2

Benedick Pray thee, sweet Mistress Margaret, deserve well at my hands
by helping me to the speech of Beatrice.

Margaret Will you then write me a sonnet in praise of my beauty?

Benedick In so high a style, Margaret, that no man living shall come
over it, for in most comely truth, thou deservest it.   5

Margaret To have no man come over me, why, shall I always keep
below stairs?

Benedick Thy wit is as quick as the greyhound's mouth, it catches.

Margaret And yours as blunt as the fencer's foils, which hit but hurt not.

Benedick A most manly wit, Margaret, it will not hurt a woman. And so,   10
I pray thee call Beatrice. I give thee the bucklers.

Margaret Give us the swords. We have bucklers of our own.

Benedick If you use them, Margaret, you must put in the pikes with a vice,
and they are dangerous weapons for maids.

Margaret Well, I will call Beatrice to you, who I think hath legs.   15

Exit Margaret

Benedick And therefore will come.
[Sings] The god of love,
                That sits above,
                And knows me, and knows me,
                How pitiful I deserve—   20
I mean in singing. But in loving, Leander, the good swimmer,
Troilus the first employer of panders and a whole book full of
these quondam carpet-mongers, whose names yet run smoothly
in the even road of a blank verse, why they were never so truly
turned over and over as my poor self in love. Marry, I cannot   25

Beatrice comes in and Benedick tells her that he has challenged Claudio to a duel as she asked him to. They discuss their feelings for each other.

Beatrice and Benedick, 2012

Activity 2: Exploring a battle of wits

a. In pairs, read aloud lines 31–39 with one of you as Benedick and the other as Beatrice.

b. On your feet, read the lines again. This time the person playing Benedick should start by holding an object such as a pencil case or a bottle of water and the person playing Beatrice must take the object as they speak their own line. Continue taking the object from each other throughout lines 31–39. The person holding the object can make it easy or difficult for the other person to take it.

c. Discuss and note down the moments at which you grabbed the object and how that happened.

d. Make a list of words to describe Beatrice and Benedick's behaviour. Use this vocabulary to write a paragraph or two explaining how Beatrice and Benedick communicate during lines 31–39.

Glossary

27 **innocent** simple
30 **festival terms** flowery language
39 **is noisome** stinks
43 **subscribe him** make a signed statement that he is
45 **so politic a** such a well-organised
49 **epithet** expression
51 **spite it** irritate it

show it in rhyme, I have tried. I can find out no rhyme to 'lady'
but 'baby', an innocent rhyme; for 'scorn' 'horn', a hard rhyme;
for 'school' 'fool', a babbling rhyme: very ominous endings. No,
I was not born under a rhyming planet, nor I cannot woo in
festival terms.   30

Enter Beatrice

Sweet Beatrice, wouldst thou come when I called thee?

Beatrice   Yea, signor, and depart when you bid me.

Benedick   O, stay but till then.

Beatrice   'Then' is spoken. Fare you well now. And yet ere I go, let me
go with that I came, which is with knowing what hath passed   35
between you and Claudio.

Benedick   Only foul words, and thereupon I will kiss thee.

Beatrice   Foul words is but foul wind, and foul wind is but foul breath,
and foul breath is noisome, therefore I will depart unkissed.

Benedick   Thou hast frighted the word out of his right sense, so forcible   40
is thy wit. But I must tell thee plainly, Claudio undergoes my
challenge and either I must shortly hear from him, or I will
subscribe him a coward. And I pray thee now tell me for which
of my bad parts didst thou first fall in love with me?

Beatrice   For them all together, which maintained so politic a state of   45
evil that they will not admit any good part to intermingle with
them. But for which of my good parts did you first suffer love
for me?

Benedick   'Suffer love!' A good epithet. I do suffer love indeed, for I love
thee against my will.   50

Beatrice   In spite of your heart, I think. Alas, poor heart. If you spite it for
my sake I will spite it for yours, for I will never love that which
my friend hates.

Benedick   Thou and I are too wise to woo peaceably.

Beatrice   It appears not in this confession. There's not one wise man   55
among twenty that will praise himself.

ula comes in to ask Beatrice to go to see Leonato because there is proof that Don John
ceived Don Pedro and Claudio, and that Hero was falsely accused. Beatrice asks Benedick
go with her, to which he agrees.

Benedick and Beatrice, 2014

Activity 3: Exploring character

a. In pairs, read aloud lines 73–76 with one of you as Ursula and the other listening as Beatrice.

b. Write a sentence that explains how Beatrice feels when she hears the news.

c. Write down three questions that Beatrice might have when she hears the news.

d. Swap roles and read lines 73–76 again.

e. Write a sentence that explains how Benedick feels when he hears the news.

f. Write down three questions that Benedick might have when he hears the news.

g. Discuss the differences between Benedick's and Beatrice's response to this news. What does the photo on this page suggest about their different responses?

Glossary

57 **instance** argument

59 **in monument** in remembrance

62 **Question** good question

62 **rheum** tears

63 **Don Worm** The worm is a traditional image for conscience

73 **old coil** much confusion

75 **abused** deceived

76 **presently** immediately

Benedick An old, an old instance, Beatrice, that lived in the time of good
neighbours. If a man do not erect in this age his own tomb ere
he dies, he shall live no longer in monument than the bell rings
and the widow weeps.   60

Beatrice And how long is that, think you?

Benedick Question: why, an hour in clamour and a quarter in rheum.
Therefore is it most expedient for the wise, if Don Worm his
conscience find no impediment to the contrary, to be the
trumpet of his own virtues, as I am to myself. So much for   65
praising myself who, I myself will bear witness, is praiseworthy.
And now tell me, how doth your cousin?

Beatrice Very ill.

Benedick And how do you?

Beatrice Very ill too.   70

Benedick Serve God, love me and mend. There will I leave you too, for
here comes one in haste.

Enter Ursula

Ursula Madam, you must come to your uncle, yonder's old coil at
home. It is proved my Lady Hero hath been falsely accused,
the Prince and Claudio mightily abused, and Don John is the   75
author of all, who is fled and gone. Will you come presently?

Beatrice Will you go hear this news, signor?

Benedick I will live in thy heart, die in thy lap, and be buried in thy eyes.
And moreover I will go with thee to thy uncle's.

Exeunt

That night, Claudio, Don Pedro, Balthasar and servants come to mourn Hero. Claudio delivers his epitaph for Hero. Balthasar sings a song for her and Claudio promises to remember Hero with an annual ceremony. Dawn breaks and Don Pedro dismisses the assembly.

Claudio and servants, 2006

At the time

Using page 207, find out about the traditions of mourning in Elizabethan times.

Activity 1: Exploring Hero's epitaph

a. In pairs, read aloud lines 3–8, swapping readers at the end of each line.

b. The words at the ends of the lines rhyme. Why do you think Shakespeare presents lines 7 and 8 as a **rhyming couplet**?

c. Create a freeze-frame that shows the moment when Claudio shamed Hero at the altar.

d. Create a freeze-frame that shows Claudio celebrating Hero in 'glorious fame'.

e. Create a third freeze-frame that shows Hero the way you think she should be remembered.

f. Discuss what the freeze-frames show about Hero's character.

g. Write your own six-line **epitaph** for Hero, using the same rhyming pattern as Shakespeare does, ending with a rhyming couplet.

Glossary

1 **monument** family tomb
5 **guerdon** payment
12 **goddess of the night** Diana, the moon goddess, protector of virgins
20 **utterèd** expressed
26 **wheels of Phoebus** chariot of the sun god

Key terms

Rhyming couplet two lines of verse where the last words of each line rhyme

Epitaph something written or said in memory of a dead person

Act 5 | Scene 3

Enter Claudio, Don Pedro, Balthasar and attendants

Claudio Is this the monument of Leonato?

Lord It is, my lord.

Claudio [Reads the epitaph] 'Done to death by slanderous tongues
Was the Hero that here lies.
Death, in guerdon of her wrongs,   5
Gives her fame which never dies.
So the life that died with shame
Lives in death with glorious fame.'
Hang thou there upon the tomb,
Praising her when I am dumb.   10
Now, music sound, and sing your solemn hymn.

Balthasar [Sings] Pardon, goddess of the night,
Those that slew thy virgin knight,
For the which, with songs of woe
Round about her tomb they go.   15
Midnight, assist our moan.
Help us to sigh and groan,
Heavily, heavily.
Graves, yawn and yield your dead,
Till death be utterèd,   20
Heavily, heavily.

Claudio Now, unto thy bones good night
Yearly will I do this rite.

Don Pedro Good morrow, masters, put your torches out.
The wolves have preyed, and look, the gentle day   25
Before the wheels of Phoebus round about
Dapples the drowsy east with spots of grey.
Thanks to you all, and leave us. Fare you well.

Activity 2: Exploring setting

a. Imagine you are in Leonato's family tomb. Write down something you would be able to see in the tomb in as much detail as you can, using **adjectives** in your description. If you need inspiration, look at the photo on this page.

b. Do the same for:
   i. the sound of something you could hear in the tomb
   ii. the smell of something in the tomb
   iii. the texture of something that you would be able to touch in the tomb.

c. Describe the temperature and atmosphere in the tomb.

d. Share and discuss what you have written.

e. Use these ideas as inspiration to help you write a detailed description of the setting for Act 5 Scene 3.

Ursula, Balthasar, Claudio, Don Pedro, Margaret and servants, 2014

Glossary

29 **several** separate
30 **weeds** clothes
32 **Hymen** god of marriage
32 **issue speeds** outcome help us
33 **woe** grief

Key term

Adjective a word that describes a noun, e.g. *blue, happy, big*

Did you know?

The designer of an RSC production creates a multi-sensory world in which the action of the play can take place. They consider every detail to create the richest and most appropriate setting that they can.

Claudio   Good morrow, masters, each his several way.

Don Pedro   Come, let us hence, and put on other weeds.   30
                And then to Leonato's we will go.

Claudio   And Hymen now with luckier issue speeds
                Than this for whom we rendered up this woe.

                Exeunt

Next day, Leonato and his family, with Friar Francis and Benedick, get ready for Claudio and Don Pedro to come. The women go into a side room to put on masks. Benedick asks the Friar if he will marry him to Beatrice.

Leonato and Benedick, 2014

Activity 1: Exploring the theme of love

a. In groups, decide who will play Leonato, Benedick and the Friar. Read aloud lines 18–32.

b. Read the lines again, but this time whisper them as if the characters are talking about something secret and do not want to be overheard.

c. Stand about five steps apart and read the lines again, loudly.

d. Discuss how these different ways of reading the lines change your understanding of the scene.

e. Finally, read the lines again, this time varying the volume of your speech according to how you think the scene should be performed.

f. Do you think Benedick genuinely wants to marry Beatrice? To what extent is his request simply a way of Shakespeare ending the play in the traditional way? Write a paragraph or two explaining your answer in detail, using evidence from earlier in the play.

Glossary

6 **question** investigation
8 **faith** honour
14 **office** function
17 **confirmed countenance** a straight face
18 **pains** work
20 **undo** ruin; release

At the time

Using page 202, find out what was the traditional ending of a comedy and why.

182

Act 5 | Scene 4

Enter Leonato, Antonio, Benedick, Beatrice, Margaret, Ursula, Friar and Hero

Friar   Did I not tell you she was innocent?

Leonato   So are the Prince and Claudio who accused her
Upon the error that you heard debated.
But Margaret was in some fault for this,
Although against her will as it appears   5
In the true course of all the question.

Antonio   Well, I am glad that all things sort so well.

Benedick   And so am I, being else by faith enforced
To call young Claudio to a reckoning for it.

Leonato   Well, daughter, and you gentlewomen all,   10
Withdraw into a chamber by yourselves,
And when I send for you come hither masked.
The Prince and Claudio promised by this hour
To visit me. You know your office, brother:
You must be father to your brother's daughter,   15
And give her to young Claudio.

Exeunt Beatrice, Hero, Margaret and Ursula

Antonio   Which I will do with confirmed countenance.

Benedick   Friar, I must entreat your pains, I think.

Friar   To do what, signor?

Benedick   To bind me, or undo me, one of them.   20
Signor Leonato, truth it is, good signor,
Your niece regards me with an eye of favour.

Leonato   That eye my daughter lent her, 'tis most true.

Benedick   And I do with an eye of love requite her.

Don Pedro and Claudio arrive so that Claudio can be married to Leonato's 'niece' and fulfil his contract to Leonato's family. Antonio goes out to fetch the bride. He brings back Hero, Beatrice, Margaret and Ursula, all wearing masks.

Claudio and the masked women, 2006

Activity 2: Exploring Claudio

a. Discuss the photo on this page, which shows Claudio facing masked women from the 2006 RSC production.
   i. What is the expression of the masks and why do you think that is?
   ii. What colour are the women wearing and what does that suggest?
   iii. All the women are identical. How does this, and their pose, help us to understand the choice that Claudio is making at this point in the action?
b. Create a **statue** of Claudio in line 53. Read the line aloud to bring your statue to life.
c. Write a sentence in modern English describing what Claudio might be thinking and feeling in line 53.
d. Why do you think Claudio is so determined to marry Leonato's niece, despite having never met her? Do you think his determination makes him more honourable or less honourable? Give reasons for your answer.

Glossary

38 **an Ethiope** dark-skinned

43–47 **savage bull...**
   love In a mythological story Jupiter, king of the gods, transforms himself into a bull and carries off Princess Europa

44 **horns** cuckold's horns

45 **all Europa** the entire continent of Europe

46 **Europa** Princess Europa

Key term

statue like a freeze-frame but usually of a single character

Leonato   The sight whereof I think you had from me,   25
From Claudio and the Prince. But what's your will?

Benedick   Your answer, sir, is enigmatical.
But, for my will, my will is your good will
May stand with ours this day to be conjoined
In the state of honourable marriage,   30
In which, good Friar, I shall desire your help.

Leonato   My heart is with your liking.

Friar   And my help.
Here comes the Prince and Claudio.

Enter Don Pedro and Claudio with attendants

Don Pedro   Good morrow to this fair assembly.

Leonato   Good morrow, Prince. Good morrow, Claudio.   35
We here attend you. Are you yet determined
Today to marry with my brother's daughter?

Claudio   I'll hold my mind, were she an Ethiope.

Leonato   Call her forth, brother, here's the Friar ready.

Exit Antonio

Don Pedro   Good morrow, Benedick. Why, what's the matter   40
That you have such a February face,
So full of frost, of storm and cloudiness?

Claudio   I think he thinks upon the savage bull.
Tush, fear not, man, we'll tip thy horns with gold,
And all Europa shall rejoice at thee   45
As once Europa did at lusty Jove
When he would play the noble beast in love.

Benedick   Bull Jove, sir, had an amiable low,
And some such strange bull leaped your father's cow
And got a calf in that same noble feat   50
Much like to you, for you have just his bleat.

Enter Antonio with Hero, Beatrice, Margaret and Ursula, masked

Claudio is offered one of the masked women by Antonio, as if she is his daughter. Claudio asks to see her face, but Leonato insists he marry her without seeing her. After he agrees, the woman unmasks and is revealed as Hero. In front of everyone, Benedick asks Beatrice if she loves him.

Activity 3: Exploring the unmasking of Hero

a. Read lines 58–66 and discuss the following questions:
   i. What do you think is the exact moment when Hero's mask comes off?
   ii. Do you think Hero takes her own mask off or does someone else do it for her?
   iii. How do you think Hero should speak her lines in this section and why?
b. Stand up and read lines 58–66 again, this time including your ideas for unmasking Hero.
c. Write a sentence explaining what you think is going through Hero's mind in line 66.
d. Share your sentences and discuss how you think things will work out for Hero and Claudio.
e. Write a summary of what happens in lines 58–66 from Hero's point of view.

Glossary

67 **qualify** explain
68 **holy rites** marriage ceremony
69 **largely** fully
71 **presently** immediately
72 **Soft and fair** gently

Hero, Ursula, Margaret and Claudio, 2014

Claudio For this I owe you. Here comes other reck'nings.
Which is the lady I must seize upon?

Antonio This same is she, and I do give you her.

Claudio Why then, she's mine. Sweet, let me see your face.   55

Leonato No, that you shall not till you take her hand
Before this Friar and swear to marry her.

Claudio Give me your hand before this holy friar.
I am your husband, if you like of me.

Hero And when I lived, I was your other wife.   60
And when you loved, you were my other husband.

Hero unmasks

Claudio Another Hero?

Hero   Nothing certainer.
One Hero died defiled, but I do live,
And surely as I live, I am a maid.

Don Pedro The former Hero, Hero that is dead!   65

Leonato She died, my lord, but whiles her slander lived.

Friar All this amazement can I qualify
When after that the holy rites are ended
I'll tell you largely of fair Hero's death.
Meantime let wonder seem familiar,   70
And to the chapel let us presently.

Benedick Soft and fair, Friar, which is Beatrice?

Beatrice unmasks

Beatrice I answer to that name. What is your will?

Benedick Do not you love me?

Beatrice   Why no, no more than reason.

Benedick Why then, your uncle and the Prince and Claudio   75
Have been deceived: they swore you did.

Benedick and Beatrice say they do not love each other, but Claudio produces proof in the form of a love poem that Benedick has written for Beatrice and Hero produces one that Beatrice has written for Benedick. Benedick asks Beatrice to marry him and she agrees.

Activity 4: Exploring how private or public a moment is

a. In pairs, read aloud lines 74–83 with one of you as Benedick and the other as Beatrice.

b. Read the lines again, but this time whisper the lines as if Benedick and Beatrice do not want to be overheard by the other characters. How does this change the moment?

c. Form two small groups: one group of people who have been playing Beatrice and the other of people who have been playing Benedick. Each group should choose one person to read the lines for their character.

d. The chosen 'Beatrice' and 'Benedick' should read lines 74–83 again, but this time the other people in their group should act as friends of that character, supporting what they say with cheers and other sounds and gestures. Benedick and Beatrice should use their friends' support as they speak. How does this change the moment?

e. Discuss why you think Beatrice and Benedick deny that they love each other.

f. If you were going to stage this moment, how private or public would you make it? Give reasons for your answer.

Beatrice and Benedick, 2012

Glossary

83 **recompense** compensation
87 **halting** limping; not flowing
99 **satire** sarcastic ridicule
100 **epigram** short, witty saying
100 **a shall** he shall
101 **handsome** fashionable

Did you know?

Shakespeare's plays were first performed in theatres where the audience surrounded three sides of the stage. This meant that even when there were other characters on stage, two or three characters could have a private moment between themselves. In rehearsals, actors have to work out the extent to which those moments are private or public, as part of blocking a scene.

Beatrice Do not you love me?

Benedick   Troth no, no more than reason.

Beatrice Why, then my cousin, Margaret, and Ursula
Are much deceived, for they did swear you did.

Benedick They swore that you were almost sick for me.   80

Beatrice They swore that you were well-nigh dead for me.

Benedick 'Tis no such matter. Then you do not love me?

Beatrice No, truly, but in friendly recompense.

Leonato Come, cousin, I am sure you love the gentleman.

Claudio And I'll be sworn upon't that he loves her,   85
For here's a paper written in his hand,
A halting sonnet of his own pure brain,
Fashioned to Beatrice.

Hero   And here's another
Writ in my cousin's hand, stolen from her pocket,
Containing her affection unto Benedick.   90

Benedick A miracle, here's our own hands against our hearts. Come, I will
have thee, but by this light, I take thee for pity.

Beatrice I would not deny you, but by this good day, I yield upon great
persuasion and partly to save your life, for I was told you were
in a consumption.   95

Benedick Peace, I will stop your mouth.

Benedick kisses Beatrice

Don Pedro How dost thou, Benedick, the married man?

Benedick I'll tell thee what, Prince, a college of wit-crackers cannot flout
me out of my humour. Dost thou think I care for a satire or
an epigram? No, if a man will be beaten with brains, a shall   100
wear nothing handsome about him. In brief, since I do purpose
to marry, I will think nothing to any purpose that the world

Benedick advises Claudio to love Hero and says that he and Claudio are friends. He suggests a dance before the double wedding to come. A messenger comes with the news that Don John has been taken prisoner, but Benedick urges Don Pedro to forget about his brother till the next day. Everybody dances.

The wedding party, 2014

Activity 5: Exploring the themes at the end

a. In pairs, read aloud lines 108–114 with one person as Claudio and the other as Benedick.

b. Do you think Benedick really means it when he says, 'Come, come, we are friends' in line 112? Discuss the ways in which the events of the play might have changed the relationship between Benedick and Claudio.

c. Look at the photo on this page, which shows the end of the play from the 2014 RSC production. Why do you think Shakespeare ends the play with a dance? If you were going to stage the final dance, who would dance with whom, and why? Would everyone join in or would you have any characters who did not dance? If so, what would those characters be doing in the final moments of the play?

d. Write a paragraph or two explaining what you think the final moments of the action should be. You should explain how the choices you have made help to show the themes of the play: honour, loyalty, love and marriage, deception, and male and female relationships.

Glossary

103 **flout** mock
104 **giddy** inconstant
110 **double dealer** unfaithful husband
117 **staff** a symbol of authority
117 **reverend** respected
118 **horn** cuckold's horn; the risk for a married man
121 **brave** fine

Key term

Symbol a thing that represents or stands for something else

can say against it, and therefore never flout at me for what I
have said against it. For man is a giddy thing and this is my
conclusion. For thy part, Claudio, I did think to have beaten   105
thee, but in that thou art like to be my kinsman, live unbruised
and love my cousin.

Claudio I had well hoped thou wouldst have denied Beatrice, that I
might have cudgelled thee out of thy single life to make thee a
double dealer, which out of question thou wilt be, if my cousin   110
do not look exceedingly narrowly to thee.

Benedick Come, come, we are friends. Let's have a dance ere we are
married, that we may lighten our own hearts and our wives'
heels.

Leonato We'll have dancing afterward.   115

Benedick First, of my word, therefore play, music. Prince, thou art sad, get
thee a wife, get thee a wife. There is no staff more reverend than
one tipped with horn.

Enter Messenger

Messenger My lord, your brother John is ta'en in flight,
And brought with armèd men back to Messina.   120

Benedick Think not on him till tomorrow, I'll devise thee brave
punishments for him. Strike up, pipers.

Dance

Exeunt omnes

Exploring Act 5

Activity 1: Exploring the end of the play

In groups, look back over Act 5, remembering all the things that have happened. Use the page summaries to help you. Remind yourself of the key points that have happened earlier in the play as well. Imagine that the events of Act 5 have taken place now and the double wedding is to be featured on the television news. Your job is to produce that television news feature.

- Choose two people to be the presenters of the programme and one person to be a reporter on location at the wedding. The rest of you can be characters from the play.
- You should report on the wedding itself, but your programme must include as much detail as possible about what has happened in the play and interviews with the characters of your choice. You must include a variety of characters with different points of view and use quotations from the play.
- Put your programme together to share with the rest of your class.

Beatrice and Benedick, 2006

Activity 2: Exploring the themes of the play

a. Choose one of the following themes:
   - love and marriage
   - male and female relationships
   - deception
   - loyalty
   - honour.
   i. Look back over Act 5 and trace how ideas about your chosen theme have been developed and resolved in this act.
   ii. Identify the characters who are linked to this theme and explore how their words and actions express ideas about it.
b. Either prepare a presentation or write an essay about your chosen theme, entitled 'How is the theme of _____ successfully concluded in Act 5?'

Hero and Claudio, 2014

Exploring the play

Beatrice, Hero and maid, 2012

Activity 1: Assessing the relevance of the play

Look at the photos on pages 194–195, taken from Act 1 Scene 1. In this production, the **director** chose to set the play in modern-day Delhi. In the first photo, Hero and Margaret are upstairs in Hero's bedroom wearing Western dress. This was the opening moments before the dialogue of Act 1 Scene 1 started. However, in order to come down to the public part of the house to be with her father and greet their guests, Hero changed into traditional Indian dress, as in the second photo (page 195). The director wanted the audience to experience Shakespeare's play in a modern context and explore the themes of the play in our world now.

a. Discuss the following questions:

   i. Which of the things that happen to Hero in the play could happen now? Why do you think that?

   ii. What do we learn about relationships within families and between friends through studying this play?

   iii. What do you think is the main message of this play?

   iv. Why do you think the play is considered to be worth studying in this day and age?

b. Following your discussion, write an essay with the title: 'How is Shakespeare's play *Much Ado About Nothing* still relevant today?' Use the questions in task a above to structure your essay into four paragraphs.

Activity 2: Exploring the theme of deception

a. Write a list of all the deceptions that happen in
   Much Ado About Nothing, including well-intended
   deceptions as well as those that are intended to
   cause harm.
b. Taking each deception in turn, discuss:
   i. why you think Shakespeare included it in
       the play
   ii. how you think the audience would react to
       that deception.
c. Design a mask for one of the characters to wear in
   Act 2 Scene 1. The mask must be designed to show
   what that character is like and what their role is in
   the play.
d. Write notes that explain your design, including at
   least three lines from the play in your answer.

Shakespeare's life

William Shakespeare is probably the most famous playwright of all time. Here's a summary of his life, his work and important events at the time.

1564

William Shakespeare is born in Stratford-upon-Avon.

1595

Romeo and Juliet and A Midsummer Night's Dream first performed.

1593

Shakespeare's first published work, the poem Venus and Adonis.

1592–3

The London theatres close for several months because of a plague outbreak.

1596

The Merchant of Venice first performed.

1596

Hamnet Shakespeare dies and is buried in Stratford-upon-Avon.

1597

Shakespeare buys a large house, New Place, in Stratford-upon-Avon.

1608

Death of Shakespeare's mother, Mary.

1606

Macbeth first performed.

1605

The Gunpowder Plot, a threat to blow up the king in Parliament, fails. ➤

1611

The Tempest first performed.

1611

The King James Bible, or Authorized Version, is published.

1613

Shakespeare's last plays, The Two Noble Kinsmen and Henry VIII, both jointly written with John Fletcher, are performed.

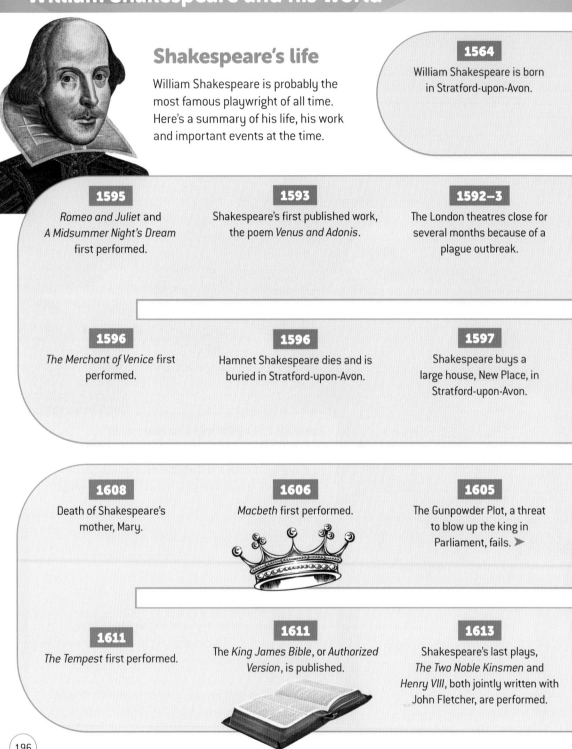

1582

He marries Anne Hathaway.

1583

Susanna Shakespeare, William and Anne's first child, is born.

1585

Two more children, the twins Hamnet and Judith, are born.

1592

By this date Shakespeare had begun his career in London as an actor and playwright. A rival, Robert Greene, described him in print as an 'upstart crow'.

1588

◀ Spanish Armada is defeated.

1598

Much Ado About Nothing first performed.

1599

Shakespeare's theatre company builds the Globe theatre in London. ➤

1603

Death of Queen Elizabeth. The new king, James I, takes over the patronage of Shakespeare's company and they are renamed the King's Men.

1601

Death of Shakespeare's father, John.

1616

Shakespeare dies in Stratford-upon-Avon and is buried in a local church.

1623

The first collected edition of his plays, the *First Folio*, is published in London. ➤

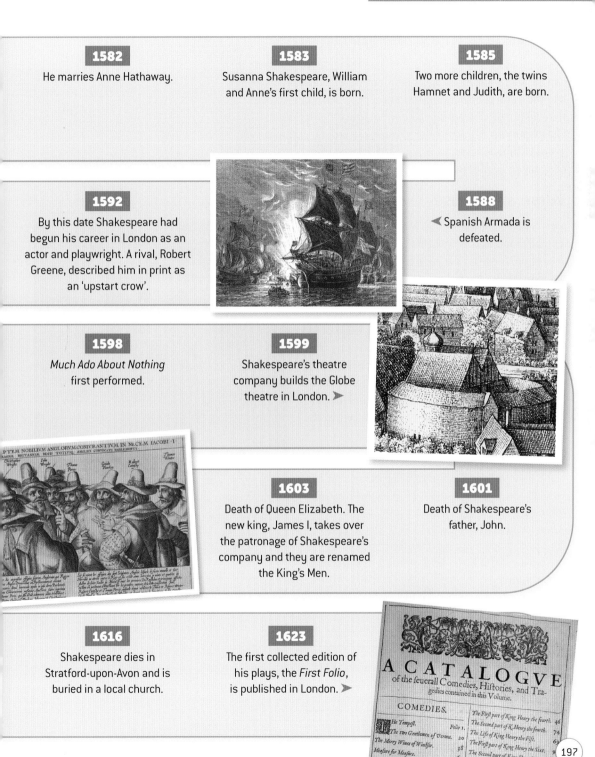

Shakespeare's language

Shakespeare's language can be difficult for us to understand for two different reasons. One is historical: words and their meanings, and the ways people express themselves, have changed over the four hundred years since he wrote. The other is poetic: Shakespeare's characters don't speak like ordinary people, even in the Elizabethan period, would have spoken. They speak in a heightened, poetic language full of repetition and elaboration.

Verse and prose

Most Shakespeare plays are written in verse with a small proportion of prose included. You can tell verse from prose on the page because verse lines are usually shorter and each line begins with a capital letter, whereas prose lines usually begin with lower-case letters (unless it is the beginning of a sentence) and continue to the very edge of the paper. Verse is a more formal way of speaking and is often associated with higher-status characters, whereas servants or other lower-class figures more often speak prose. Comic scenes are sometimes in prose, where the language is more relaxed and natural.

Beatrice (top), Hero and Ursula, 2014

Shakespeare's verse is often called blank verse – blank means it does not rhyme. But occasionally he does use rhyme, sometimes in a couplet (two rhyming lines) at the end of a scene to signal that it has come to a conclusion or as a character exits. For example, here are the lines Hero speaks as she leaves the stage in Act 3 Scene 1 of *Much Ado About Nothing*:

> **Hero** If it proves so, then loving goes by haps.
> Some Cupid kills with arrows, some with traps.

At other times, Shakespeare uses rhyme to suggest formality. Rhyming lines were probably easier for actors to learn.

Iambic pentameter

Poetry — like music — is words ordered into rhythm. The metre of poetry is like its drumbeat. Most of Shakespeare's verse lines are written in iambic pentameter. A pentameter means that there are five beats to the line (and usually ten syllables); iambic means that the beats are alternately weak and strong, or unstressed and stressed.

An example from *Much Ado About Nothing* is when Claudio rejects Hero at their wedding and addresses her father, Leonato. The numbers below the line count the syllables; the marks below the numbers show that the syllables alternate between unstressed (signalled with -) and stressed (/). It looks more complicated when you write it down than when you read it aloud.

Claudio	Give not this rotten orange to your friend.
	1 2 3 4 5 6 7 8 9 10
	- / - / - / - / - /

As with music, the sound of Shakespeare's language would get repetitive if he never varied the rhythm. So sometimes he changes the arrangement of stressed and unstressed syllables, and sometimes lines can be read with different emphases depending on the actor's interpretation. Reading Shakespeare's lines aloud often helps.

One clue: often Shakespeare puts important words or ideas at the end of his lines, rather than at the beginning. If you look down a speech and look at the last word in each line you can usually get some idea of the main point of the speech. One additional clue: with longer speeches, often the beginning and the end are the most important, and the middle says the same thing in different ways.

Shakespeare's world

Knowing something about life in Shakespeare's England is often helpful for our understanding of his plots and characters, and of the assumptions that members of his audiences would have had when they went to see his plays. But it is also important to remember that he was an imaginative playwright, making up stories for entertainment.

Just as we wouldn't necessarily rely on modern Hollywood films or television drama to depict our everyday reality, so too we need sometimes to acknowledge that Shakespeare is showing his audiences something exotic, unfamiliar or fairy tale.

London and the theatres

At some point in his early twenties, Shakespeare moved from the country town of Stratford to London. Thousands of people at the time did the same, moving to the city for work and other opportunities, and London expanded rapidly during the Elizabethan period. It was a busy, commercial place that had outgrown the original walled city and was now organised around the main thoroughfare, the river Thames. Shakespeare never sets a play in contemporary London, although many of his urban locations, particularly Venice, seem to recall the inns and streets and bustle of the city in which he and his audiences lived and worked.

17th-century engraving of London by Claes Jansz Visscher

As a port city, London was a place where people from different places mixed together, although its society was much less racially diverse than now. Jews had been banned from England in the medieval period, although there were some secret communities in London, so almost no one in Shakespeare's England would ever have met a Jewish person. A visit of Arab ambassadors from North Africa to Queen Elizabeth's court in 1600 must have seemed very exotic indeed.

The audience for Shakespeare's plays was quite mixed, but probably tended to be younger rather than older and male rather than female. Types of entertainment such as romantic comedy, that are now mainly associated with female audiences, were then directed at male theatregoers. Entry to the theatres was cheap – one penny, the cost of two pints of beer – so a relatively diverse social mix could attend. We don't know how well-educated the audience was, although educational opportunities were expanding during the 16th century and historians think that the number of men who were able to read and write in London at this point may have been as high as 50%. Literacy was connected to social status: wealthier individuals were much more likely to be educated than poorer ones. Laughing at unlearned people and their mistakes in language is a common source of comedy in Shakespeare's plays: we don't know how many of the people laughing were themselves not well-educated.

The Watch

Elizabethan England had no police force. Instead, the Watch was an amateur force of local men who agreed to serve their community for a fixed term, to keep order and patrol the night streets. Their job was to look out for thieves, to stop fights and to keep a watch for fires. Shakespeare's father John served as a constable in the Stratford Watch when his son was a child.

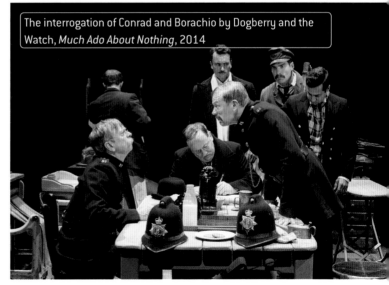

The interrogation of Conrad and Borachio by Dogberry and the Watch, *Much Ado About Nothing*, 2014

Comedy and tragedy

For us, a comedy is something funny. In Shakespeare's time, comedy had those associations too, but more importantly it was defined by the shape of the story. A comedy had a happy ending, in which characters were united, social bonds reaffirmed and things were better than they were at the beginning. A tragedy was the opposite: the central tragic character (often the play is named after them) becomes more and more isolated and is destroyed in a plot where things are definitely worse at the end than at the beginning. One of Shakespeare's fellow playwrights, Thomas Heywood, defined comedy and tragedy: 'comedies begin in trouble and end in peace; tragedies begin in calms and end in tempest'.

Comedies traditionally ended with reunion or with marriage. Those elements that had kept the couple apart during the play – sometimes these are external factors such as a disapproving parent, sometimes more psychological factors such as an unwillingness to commit – are overcome. The final scene of a comedy tends to bring together all its characters and reconcile all the plots. The suggestion is that the new couples will bring about new life and the regeneration of the community.

Mercutio in disguise, *Romeo and Juliet*, 2006

Masks

We don't know how popular masked parties or balls were in Elizabethan England, but Shakespeare makes use of them in his plays because they allow usual social conventions to be lifted. Under the cover of a mask, characters can speak their true thoughts or can have unusual access to other characters (particularly of the opposite sex) in disguise. In combining disguise with music and costumes, the masked ball is like the play itself: a space for characters to find out new things about themselves and each other.

Fate and the planets

Many people in Elizabethan England believed in horoscopes and the idea that the position of the planets at the time of birth influenced the child's future life. Astronomical events like solar or lunar eclipses or comets visible in the sky were often understood to be signs or portents. The planets were also thought to have a role in disease: the word 'influenza' (from which we get the abbreviation 'flu') comes from the Latin for 'astrological influence'. These older, more superstitious attitudes to the planets co-existed in Shakespeare's lifetime with new scientific discoveries, including Galileo's telescope and observations of the planets by other astronomers.

Don Armado and Moth, *Love's Labour's Lost*, 1946

Claudio and Hero, *Much Ado About Nothing*, 1950

Love

Romantic love had been a prominent literary theme for centuries. Courtly love traditions tended to present an idealised female figure who ignored her suffering admirer; romantic stories tended to end in disappointment or worse. Love was considered to be a random emotion (in contrast to the arranged marriages discussed under 'marriage and courtship' on pages 204–205). The symbolism of the blindfolded god of love, Cupid, was clear: Love did not care where his arrows fell, creating mayhem in the world by making people fall in love with each other. The goddess of sexual love, Venus, was well-known in Elizabethan literature: one of Shakespeare's earliest works is a long poem, *Venus and Adonis*, which flips the usual story for comic effect and shows the goddess longing for a young man who is not interested in her.

A person in love was often thought to show symptoms of melancholy or depression, and to withdraw from company, particularly of the same sex. Enjoying love poetry or other romantic literature, or the company of women (for men) might also be a sign of being in love.

Women

Ideas about the ideal woman are current in many societies, including modern ones. Just as we know that most real women now do not conform to the thin, beautiful, youthful ideal of modern advertising, so too probably Elizabethan women were different from the models given to them in conduct books, sermons and literature. The ideal woman, according to writers on morality in Shakespeare's England, remained meekly at home. She was chaste, honest, silent and obedient to her husband's will.

A moral double standard meant that women's behaviour, especially their chastity, was much more policed than that of men. Unmarried women were expected to obey their fathers and conduct themselves modestly. Women did not attend school or university, although wealthy ones might be educated at home. Except for widows, women could not hold property in their own right. But alongside these stereotypes there were many exceptional women, from Queen Elizabeth to the writer Mary Sidney and the pirate Mary Killigrew, as well as ordinary women living, working and running their households.

Rose Oatley, Sir Hugh Lacy and Rowland Lacy, *The Shoemaker's Holiday*, 2014

Marriage and courtship

Elizabethan marriages tended to be seen as alliances between families, as much as between the couple themselves. In wealthy or noble families, a suitable marriage arranged between the parents of the couple was common; for ordinary people, there may have been more possibility to choose a partner, although parental permission was still important. Marriage was a practical commitment rather than, or as well as, a romantic partnership: perhaps couples then did not place such high emotional expectations on their married relationships as in modern western societies. Some high-born people might be engaged as children, but the age of consent was 21 (Shakespeare needed his father's permission to marry aged just 18). Most Elizabethan brides and grooms were in their mid-twenties when they married.

Weddings could happen in church, but they also could be legally contracted if the couple promised to marry each other in front of a witness and then consummated their relationship. A betrothal or engagement might precede the formal marriage service: this was a legally binding commitment between the couple. The Elizabethan church marriage service suggested that marriage had three purposes: children, the avoidance of fornication, and the comfort and companionship between husband and wife. Bible verses in the service instructed husbands to love and cherish their wives, and wives to submit to their husband's authority. The couple would wear their best clothes (the tradition of a bride wearing white came later) and afterwards there would usually be feasting.

Romeo and Juliet with Friar Laurence by Mather Brown, c.1805, Royal Shakespeare Company Collection (oil on canvas)

Marriages were subject to the same problems and stresses then as now, although there was almost no divorce allowed in the Elizabethan period. Cheating on your husband or wife or being married to more than one person were seen as sins to be punished by the church courts; a clergyman who broke the rules on the correct forms of marriage would also be in serious trouble. A man whose wife was unfaithful, or rumoured to be unfaithful, was ridiculed and disrespected. He was known as a 'cuckold' and it was said that horns grew on his head.

Illegitimate children were often acknowledged within noble families – they were thought to have dark and negative personalities because they were born outside of marriage, which was considered immoral – but poor women who gave birth outside marriage were often left homeless and penniless. Lower-status women were the most vulnerable in Shakespeare's England: if a woman was thrown out by her family her prospects were very harsh indeed.

Children

In the Elizabethan period, children were expected to obey their parents, wives their husbands, and servants their masters. Consequences of disobedience could be very serious. Children in higher-class families often lived with relatives or were quite distant from their parents; for lower-status families, young children would be expected to work in the household. It is likely that the young Shakespeare would have helped out in his father's workshop. Young children in noble families wore the same clothes for both sexes until a ceremony called 'breeching' when boys began to wear breeches (trousers), aged about 7.

Duelling and sword fights

Being able to handle a sword was the mark of a gentleman in Elizabethan society (servants were not allowed to carry swords). Noblemen were often quick to take offence if they were insulted, and defending their honour was sometimes a justification for a challenge to a duel – a single combat with weapons. However common it might have been, duelling was actually illegal in Elizabethan England. Shakespeare's sword fights are more to do with the theatre than with real life. They play the same role for his audiences as action sequences in modern films do for us now, placing characters in an intense encounter, often where we want one particular individual to triumph. Sword fights also give fit male actors an excuse for impressive physical display.

Edgar duels with a masked opponent, *King Lear*, 2007

Health and medicine

The Elizabethans believed in an ancient theory that saw four elements – fire, earth, air and water – reflected in four parts of the body. These were known as 'humours': yellow bile, black bile, phlegm and blood. The balance of the humours was felt to be necessary for good health and when Shakespeare uses the word 'humour' he means something like 'temperament' rather than, as now, something funny.

Elizabethan doctors – physicians – treated only the wealthiest members of society who could pay for their services. Lower down in society, surgeons might deal with injuries and barbers were licensed to take blood (to balance the humours) and pull out teeth. The most common medical practitioner for ordinary people would have been an apothecary, who sold drugs and potions. Many people made their own remedies – known as simples – from herbs and other ingredients. There was little understanding of the relationship between health and sanitation, and, when outbreaks of plague happened in London, the main response was to ban gatherings of people at the theatre and to close up or quarantine infected houses.

Honour

Behaving honourably was an important element of male and female behaviour. But male and female honour were differently understood. For men, honour was about status and about being judged by others: keeping up appearances, looking brave and manly, not being ridiculed or made to look foolish. For women, honour was about sexual conduct: to be honourable was to be chaste and to be seen to be chaste. Honourable behaviour for women was to be beyond reproach.

Death

Representations of death in the Elizabethan period often used a skeleton or a skull to suggest mortality. The image of the skeleton who is part of everyday life was key to a famous set of illustrations called the *Dance of Death*, which show how Death, complete with a scythe or other weapon, waits in every situation to take his prey. Monuments in churches often used a skull to symbolise death.

'The Abbess' from the *Dance of Death* by Hans Holbein

The dead were buried in the churchyard, with a Christian service that emphasised that the living returned to the earth from which they had originally been made: 'earth to earth, ashes to ashes', and prayed for eternal life at the day of judgement. Richer families would pay for a coffin and there might be a procession of male relatives and others following the body. The poor would be buried in a shroud or sheet. One disturbing element of the plague was that mass burials in plague pits were required to dispose of all the dead.

Mourners wore black and it was common to buy mourning rings or other mementoes to remember the dead. In his will, Shakespeare left money to three fellow actors to buy rings in his memory. Suicide was considered a sin, and those who had taken their own life were not allowed to be buried in the holy ground of the churchyard or according to the church rites.

Key terms glossary

Adjective a word that describes a noun, e.g. *blue*, *happy*, *big*

Antithesis bringing two opposing concepts or ideas together, e.g. hot and cold, love and hate, loud and quiet

Backstory what happened to any of the characters before the start of the play

Blocking the movements agreed for staging a scene

Body language how we communicate feelings to each other using our bodies (including facial expressions) rather than words

Courtship a period of time where a couple develop a romantic relationship

Dialogue a discussion between two or more people

Director the person who enables the practical and creative interpretation of a dramatic script, and ultimately brings together everybody's ideas in a way that engages the audience with the play

Dramatic climax the most intense or important point in the action of a play

Dramatic irony when the audience knows something that some characters in the play do not

Dramatic tension the anticipation of an outcome on stage, keeping the audience in suspense

Emphasis stress given to words when speaking

Epitaph something written or said in memory of a dead person

Explicit clear and open

Extended metaphor describing something by comparing it to something else over several lines

Falling action the part of a play, before the very end, in which the consequences of the dramatic climax become clear

Freeze-frame a physical, still image created by people to represent an object, place, person or feeling

Gesture a movement, often using the hands or head, to express a feeling or idea

Iambic pentameter the rhythm Shakespeare uses to write his plays. Each line in this rhythm contains approximately ten syllables. 'Iambic' means putting the stress on the second syllable of each beat. 'Pentameter' means five beats with two syllables in each beat

Imagery visually descriptive language

Improvise make up in the moment

Malapropism mistaken use of a word that sounds like another word but has a very different meaning

Monologue a long speech in which a character expresses their thoughts. Other characters may be present

Motivation a person's reason for doing something

Objective what a character wants to get or achieve in a scene

Obstacle what is in the way of a character getting what they want

Pace the speed at which someone speaks

Paraphrase put a line or section of text into your own words

Parody an imitation of a style of writing, with deliberate exaggeration to make it funny

Pronoun a word (such as *I*, *he*, *she*, *you*, *it*, *we* or *they*) that is used instead of a noun

Prop an object used in the play, e.g. a dagger

Pun a play on words

Rhyming couplet two lines of verse where the last words of each line rhyme

Soliloquy a speech in which a character is alone on stage and expresses their thoughts and feelings aloud to the audience

Stage business activity onstage

Stage direction an instruction in the text of a play, e.g. indicating which characters enter and exit a scene

Staging the process of selecting, adapting and developing the stage space in which a play will be performed

Statue like a freeze-frame but usually of a single character

Subtext the underlying meaning in the script

Syllable part of a word that is one sound, e.g. 'highness' has two syllables – 'high' and 'ness'

Symbol a thing that represents or stands for something else

Tactics the methods a character uses to get what they want

Theme the main ideas explored in a piece of literature, e.g. the themes of love and marriage, male and female relationships, deception, loyalty and honour might be considered key themes of *Much Ado About Nothing*

Tone as in 'tone of voice'; expressing an attitude through how you say something

Vowels the letters a, e, i, o, u

Woo to try to make someone fall in love with you so that they will agree to marry you